A DEDICATED VET

After an accident two years ago, medical opinion was that Gina Travers would end up in a wheelchair. Against the odds Gina had recovered and, determined to resume the veterinary career she loved, had been taken as locum at the practice owned by the attractive Ben Cassell. Gina had something to prove – to herself, and to Ben. She had to convince them both that she was up to the job. She also had to convince herself that she should ignore the attraction that was smouldering between them ... which was easier said than done.

D1513392

A DEDICATED VET

APPENDIX

A Dedicated Vet

by

Carol Wood

Dales Large Print Books
Long Preston, North Yorkshire,
BD23 4ND, England.

CORK CITY LIBRARY
WITHDRAWN FROM STOCK

British Library Cataloguing in Publication Data.

Wood, Carol
   A dedicated vet.

   A catalogue record of this book is
   available from the British Library

   ISBN   978-1-84262-517-0 pbk

First published in Great Britain 1994 by Mills & Boon Limited

Copyright © Carol Wood 1994

Cover illustration © John Hancock by arrangement with
P.W.A. International Ltd.

The moral right of the author has been asserted

Published in Large Print 2007 by arrangement with
Dorian Literary Agency

All Rights reserved. No part of this publication may be
reproduced, stored in a retrieval system, or transmitted in any
form or by any means, electronic, mechanical, photocopying,
recording or otherwise without the prior permission of the
Copyright owner.

CORK CITY LIBRARIES   5049522

Dales Large Print is an imprint of Library Magna Books Ltd.

Printed and bound in Great Britain by
T.J. (International) Ltd., Cornwall, PL28 8RW

All the characters in this book have no existence outside the imagination of the Author, and have no relation whatsoever to anyone bearing the same name or names. They are not even distantly inspired by any individual known or unknown to the Author, and all the incidents are pure invention.

CHAPTER ONE

Gina changed gear to slow in the traffic, the quay waters below the bridge very grey, lapping noiselessly against the stone walls of the harbour.

So many memories here...

Her father's words were still clear in her mind after all the years. 'Give the family business a chance, Gina, before you make up your mind on a career. You've all your life ahead of you. Don't rush into a decision.' But what her father hadn't realised was that, at sixteen, she was already committed – in her heart.

'Nothing else interests me, Dad. I want to be a vet. I just wish I could make you see!' she had argued.

'But what if you don't get your grades?' Charles Travers had invariably persisted. 'You can't even think about university without good grades.'

'I'll get them, I know I will!'

Looking back, Gina often wondered how she was so sure then, how she'd had the confidence in herself! Returning this way over the bridge, making the journey she had made so many times in her youth, brought

9

back just a glimmer of that certainty and self-assurance which had taken such a battering over the last two years.

Now at twenty-six and fully qualified, she might even have had a partnership in a practice if it hadn't been for...

Stop it, Gina! she told herself firmly as she drove. No good thinking about ifs! She hadn't given in to those sort of thoughts before and she wasn't about to start now. Focusing firmly on the road through Old Town Poole, Gina glanced in her driving mirror and caught the renewed determination in the large violet eyes which stared back at her from a face framed by dark eyebrows and soft, midnight hair drawn back into a chignon especially for the interview.

Turning the Fiesta northwards, she glanced down at the scribbled map on the dashboard. Rows of semi-detached houses slowly gave way to greener spaces and eventually she spotted the sandy lane flanked by poplars. The practice stood by itself, Ben Cassell had explained over the phone. Sure enough, about half a mile along, a curious red brick building with a kind of Dutch look to it stood adjacent to a slate-roofed cottage.

The Cassell Veterinary Clinic represented her biggest challenge yet... The advertisement in the *Veterinary Record* had been worded simply enough: 'A locum required for an indefinite period, small-animal work mostly.'

Should she have disclosed more about herself when she'd talked to him in that rather rushed call? Disappointment had followed, though, with the other job interviews when she had mentioned her period of inactivity. Who could blame her now for avoiding specific details?

Besides, what was there to lose? Only her pride! And, in the face of a refusal, at least she would feel she had done her best.

Gina climbed out of her Fiesta, breathing in the fresh air, butterflies circulating in her stomach. From her parents' place in the Purbecks it had taken longer than she thought to get here. It wasn't a journey she would care to make every day, especially at peak hours, so maybe finding a flat would be the next problem. But hey, wasn't she jumping the gun? She hadn't even met Ben Cassell yet!

'Miss Travers?'

She spun on her heel to face a man with a shock of coppery dark hair regarding her quizzically with very deeply set grey eyes.

'Yes! I'm sorry – I was miles away!'

'So it would seem. I'm Ben Cassell.' He put out a large, friendly hand and she took it. The fingers were warm in contrast to her cold ones, warm and very strong.

'You found us easily enough?' He smiled vaguely, the grey eyes skimming over her with mild interest.

'Yes, very easily. I was born in the Purbecks and I know this part of the coast pretty well. Though I have to say it's changed quite a bit – wasn't this arable land once?'

'It was, five years ago. But like much of the green belt it's been transformed by the developers... I'm almost sorry to admit the practice is part of the industrial growth.'

She shrugged lightly. 'You've managed to keep it looking very rural. There are still some fields – are they yours?'

He nodded. 'They provide a good walk for the dogs, or the odd horse or donkey who is in need of recuperation.' He gestured with a long, firm arm towards the practice. 'Come along inside. It's far warmer in the surgery.'

Gina walked beside him, aware of the penetrating look he had given her. Had he registered the slightly drawn expression which sometimes clouded her face due to the stiffness of her back? 'How long have you been here?' she asked quickly, filling in the silence.

'Just over five years. The farm had fallen victim to the economic climate and I bought it very reasonably. The buildings I converted, promising myself I wouldn't change the essential rural aspect, despite the fact that we have industrial estates just over the back there.'

Gina had a vague memory of the area as it

had been before she left home, before the light industries had sprung up. While she'd been studying in London, her life had been very full and she hadn't paid a lot of attention to the development going on in the south; mostly it was news her parents had sent her which had kept her up to date.

Now she seemed to be looking at the area with different eyes, feeling fortunate to have grown up in an environment which had managed to preserve its beauty despite the commercialism. Perhaps at twenty-six everything looked different, though. After all that happened in the last two years.

'So this was the farmhouse?' she asked, frowning at the red-brick building.

'No, the barn, believe it or not. I live next door in the original farmhouse ... the cottage there. Behind it are stables which I had converted into flats for the nurses, keeping a couple of loose-boxes for any patients we might have.'

She nodded approvingly. 'It's very unusual.'

'Come in.' He unlocked the surgery door and a faint and familiar aroma of animals and disinfectant swept out, so palpable that it made her heart beat faster with excitement. 'As it's Saturday afternoon we've no surgery so we shan't be disturbed. Go right ahead.'

He took her through the first door into a small hall and then into Reception. There were two very large rooms with modern benches and plenty of floor space, always an absolute necessity with recalcitrant animals. The windows faced south, letting in the late February sunlight, and the walls and carpeting were a subtle mixture of soft greens.

Gina liked the feel of the place instantly and would have remained longer, but Ben Cassell touched her arm lightly and led her through to the passageway. 'Consulting-rooms...' He threw open several doors as they went along. 'Dispensary, lab, recovery-rooms and prep-rooms.'

If the place had ever been a barn there was certainly no evidence of draughts or hay-lofts now. There was a sense of harmony about the place, but of keen orderliness too, which she suspected denoted a very busy practice.

'We provide adequate cover over twenty-four hours, every day of the year. If there is anything we can't take we have an arrangement with another vet in Poole and it's always worked very satisfactorily. Having said that, between ourselves and the branch practice there isn't much we can't handle.'

He stopped abruptly, urging her into a large room fitted with desktop equipment, a switchboard and, breaking the monotony, a huge cork-board flooded with newspaper cuttings and anecdotes presumably pinned there by the staff.

Gina smiled. 'I'm enjoying the tour very much, but do you think I ought to give you a little information about myself before we go any further? I mean, I might very well be wasting your time.'

'Really? And what makes you say that?' He frowned deeply, the steel-grey eyes assessing her. She had said it half as a joke to lighten the tension, but the intense pupils stared very seriously – and disconcertingly – in her direction.

She might as well get it over with. It was as good a time as any, she thought on an inner sigh. 'Mr Cassell, there was something I didn't mention in my preliminary letter, nor in my phone call to arrange this interview. I don't know if it will make any difference, but after I qualified and had taken up my first post with a practice in Surrey, I was involved in a car accident. I was in hospital for three months. Some of the nerves of my back were damaged … and it was a further year before I could walk properly.' She could see by the look on his face that he was slowly imbibing the information and hurriedly added, 'I'm quite fit now. Occasionally a bit of stiffness, but that's all.'

The perceptive eyes remained steadily on her face. He was a tall, ruggedly good-looking man, head and shoulders above her five feet seven and broad with it, dressed conservatively in a dark sports jacket and immaculate white shirt. 'Why didn't you mention this before, Miss Travers?' he asked.

'Because ... because I don't suppose you would have bothered giving me the interview, would you?'

To her dismay, he nodded. 'That may well be true.'

'I know what you're going to say,' she began, before she could stop herself, 'You want someone who is able to deal with all aspects of the job. You can't afford to have a locum who doesn't do their fair share of the heavy work. But I can assure you I certainly wouldn't have applied for the job if I didn't think I could–'

'Slow down, slow down!' He held up a large brown hand as she fell silent. 'Take a seat, Miss Travers, would you?'

She took one, the nearest, propping her bag and briefcase beside her as she folded her hands into her lap, her heart thudding. She had got this far, she must keep calm now, not panic. Give him time to digest what she had told him.

'Coffee?'

She shook her head. What if he was a man who held deeply entrenched opinions? He might not even want a woman vet full stop, although these days that particular discrimination was less ingrained...

'Don't look so worried. I appreciate your being frank with me – eventually,' he added with a sardonic grin.

She felt her cheeks flushing as she lowered her eyes. 'I'm sorry I left it so late to put you fully in the picture, but I wanted a chance to talk to you face to face.'

'You've been unsuccessful in previous job applications?'

She nodded as he came to sit at the desk. 'It's understandable from an employer's point of view, I suppose, but it's very disheartening.'

'And you're living locally?'

She shook her head. 'No, with my parents in the Purbecks temporarily until I find a position and then I'll look for a flat. Maybe something in Poole...'

'You're restricting your chances in the choice of area. I suppose you know that?'

She nodded. 'Yes, I know ... but I've made my decision to stay in the south and I'll persevere until I find something.' She took a deep breath. 'Mr Cassell, I'm certain I can do the work. I've references with me from the practice I worked for in Surrey ... before I had the accident. I spent my year of field work with them ... and eventually they offered me a position when I qualified.' She paused, adding confidently, 'Ninety per cent of the time my back doesn't give me any trouble at all, only on the odd occasion–'

'And you suggest I take a chance on the ten per cent?' he interrupted sharply.

Her face fell. 'Oh, no... I would prefer to look at it the other way...'

'It depends if you are the employer or employee, Miss Travers. As an employer I would be concerned your back might not hold out under the heavy work. A quite natural concern which it seems is validated by your previous unsuccessful attempts at finding a position.'

He was quite right, of course. She had never acted as an employer and perhaps she too would feel just as sceptical in his position.

Guardedly she reminded him, 'Your advertisement did specify small animals – not that it matters to me whether they are large or small,' she added hurriedly.

He nodded, pausing thoughtfully, then said slowly, 'We are, in the main at this practice, small-animal vets. I stated that specifically in my advertisement because my intention is to have two permanent vets here all the time. Stuart Roberts is my small-animal specialist and I want someone supporting him during the increasingly busy surgeries. This will leave Julian Lewis, my junior partner, free to concentrate on running the branch practice over at Rowhams, which is mostly large-animal work.'

'But if–'

'Please let me finish,' he interjected firmly. 'We do also have a few large-animal clients here and there has to be, as you very well know, flexibility among the staff. In other words, though the aim is towards small animals, in practice it might not turn out like that.'

'There is nothing I wouldn't attempt within reason, Mr Cassell!' Her violet eyes were determined as she added swiftly, 'Before the accident ... I was enjoying both large- and small-animal work ... look, let me show you my references...'

'No matter!' He put up a warning hand. 'I'm sure they are satisfactory. But you have been off work for a long time, haven't you? I'm sorry to be so blunt, but you're asking me to take a gamble.'

Her cheeks burned in humiliation. He wasn't even going to look at her references! He was saying the same thing as everyone else: she was too much of a risk.

'This injury? A spinal one, I take it? There's no permanent damage?' he asked, just as she had made her mind up that she was wasting her time.

'No, there's no permanent damage. The muscles have healed and, as I say, there's just stiffness occasionally.'

'There were no other complications?'

Her violet eyes grew wary. 'You mean psychologically, like losing my confidence?' Now she made no attempt to hide her annoyance. 'I might well need experience, Mr Cassell, but I invite anyone to challenge me theoretically! I'm as confident about doing my work now as I was when I qualified!'

He paused, and with a faint smile corrected her. 'I simply meant a car accident must have shaken you up very badly.'

Gina took a deep breath, thinking how 'shaken up' was rather an inadequate description of the sudden and unprecedented change in her life two years ago. At the time it had seemed like a vast black hole she couldn't even begin to crawl out of, a never-ending spiral of bad news as she'd lain in the hospital. But slowly, determinedly, she had left her dark prison behind, along with the pain of her broken relationship with Kieron Brent, the junior partner of the practice. A shudder of remembrance suddenly washed through her...

She had been so much in love with him even her physical injuries had come a poor second to the emotional trauma she'd suffered, heartbreak that she'd sworn she would never allow herself to undergo again. Mistakes like that were too costly, far too costly! But the last thing she wanted to do now was talk about those years. This was her future, the one her inner struggle had prepared her for after the bitter lesson of the past.

'Yes ... life was difficult for a while,' she admitted cautiously, unwilling to let him intimidate or unnerve her even if those wildly mesmeric eyes seemed bent on prising out the truth. 'But all that's in the past,' she added coolly. 'All I need is a chance to work again.'

'And you're expecting me to give you that chance?'

'I'm a good vet,' she answered, lifting up her chin. 'I wouldn't let you down.'

He nodded. 'I'm sure you wouldn't – intentionally. But I'll be brutally honest; I very much doubt whether you're up to the schedule. There isn't an awful lot of you, to start with!'

'That's rather a biased attitude to take, isn't it?' she bit back, flushed with anger. 'Surely size has very little to do with modern veterinary work?' She saw the hidden prejudice in those critical eyes. He meant what he said and she was suddenly more disappointed than she'd ever thought possible. 'I have no commitments,' she persevered, unwilling to resign herself to defeat. 'No domestic responsibilities, which surely must be a big factor in my favour? There's only my parents, who are busy with their own lives … it isn't as though I have to divide my time between home and work as a lot of women vets do. I just have a healthy desire to work – and to learn.'

Was he wearing down? Was he listening to her? Well, she might as well say what she

21

really felt; there was nothing to lose. 'I've learnt a lot from my past experiences, Mr Cassell. I feel more ... in tune ... with people and animals than ever before, maybe because I understand pain better. I would hope that would make a great deal of difference to my work.'

She watched him as he rose, running her eyes over the proud back, broad and erect under the jacket, the long legs moving easily under well-cut trousers. Probably she had alienated him completely with that little outburst. It hadn't sounded the way she had meant it to. Unable to bear the silence any longer, she gathered her bag and briefcase together.

'Well, thank you for seeing me, Mr Cassell. I'll find my way out.' She was in the corridor before he caught up with her, her legs feeling leaden with disappointment.

'About accommodation...' He was standing in her way, shoulders tensed. 'There's a self-contained annexe provided with the job. It's a small flat built on to the cottage, originally designed for my mother-in-law, but she's moved back to Truro. It's comfortable enough.' Then, as he paused and watched her violet eyes widen in surprise, he said with a faint smile, 'And you haven't seen the rest of the surgery yet, nor have we discussed the terms and conditions of employment.'

Caught by utter surprise at his words and the unwarranted stab of disappointment she felt on learning that Ben Cassell possessed a mother-in-law and, therefore, a wife, Gina stood stock-still. 'You mean–'

'I mean … I think we should do some more talking. Shall we dispense with formalities? Ginette, isn't it?'

Completely thrown, she stammered, 'Y-yes … it is. But to most people I'm just Gina…'

His eyes swept over her admiringly. 'Gina suits you. Very appropriate with your colouring … dark, and very beautiful.' His face did not change in expression under the shock of coppery hair. Only the slight twist of his mouth gave her any clue as to what he was thinking. Yet again she was surprised and somewhat embarrassed by this unusual man, when the serious, sombre lips broke into a full and delicious white smile.

They walked briskly to the annexe, a pretty cream stone addition built on to the cottage. She still felt stunned as the well-shaped fingers selected the correct key from a bunch of many. It was growing colder and she shivered under her warm coat, pulling up her collar.

'Tuck your head down, the lintel's low,' Ben said over his shoulder and she followed, stepping in carefully.

'Audrey … my mother-in-law … came

with us from Truro when we moved here five years ago. The place has hardly been used in the eighteen months she's been gone. Our previous locum lived with his girlfriend in Poole town and didn't need it, hence all Audrey's feminine tastes are still in evidence ... as you can see, it's definitely a woman's place.'

Gina nodded, her eyes hardly able to take in everything at once. Walking into the bay-windowed front room, she was met with a cosy assortment of plump, chintzy chairs arranged on a deep red floral carpet. They went through to a kitchen, small, but very well-equipped, and then on into the bed-room, which was furnished in much the same easy-on-the-eye style as the front room.

'It's very pretty,' Gina agreed, aware of the softening of his tone as he talked of the flat's previous occupant.

'It's centrally heated, too. Though it seems cold at the moment, once the heating is on the place is like toast. I've been meaning to have new heating put in because sometimes Audrey had problems with the plumbing. You'll have to let me know if you hear any strange noises.'

Gina smiled at his positive note. But she mustn't raise her hopes. The interview wasn't over ... yet.

'There's a small box-room along there and the garden – not that you'll be particularly interested in a garden, I suppose.'

Gina peered through the small lattice window to the neat green lawn at the back. 'On the contrary, I like gardening very much as it happens – at least, flowers and herbs.'

She straightened up and caught his lingering gaze. What was going on behind those astute grey eyes? Certainly nothing to do with gardening, she thought wryly.

Back in the front room she was suddenly very curious to find out more about this rather remote man. He was offering her a job and accommodation and yet all she knew about him was that he had a mother-in-law who had marvellous taste and was not in evidence to enjoy it!

'Your wife must miss her mother's company,' Gina said, curious to know more about the noticeably absent Mrs Ben Cassell. But she immediately wished she had been more selective about her observations as the skin of his face seemed to tighten over the high cheekbones.

'My wife died six years ago,' he told her in a perfunctory tone. 'I've never envisaged marrying again so Audrey moved here to help me with Harriet, our daughter, until she was old enough to cope. At the time, you see, she was only nine.'

The impact of his disclosure was so startling and the way in which the information was delivered so cool, it was a good few seconds before she was able to respond. 'I'm very sorry ... I had no idea!'

'Why should you? Perhaps it's better I fill you in with the facts now. The local grapevine would only provide you with a distorted version.'

'Please don't feel you have to explain–'

'Are you telling me the practice you worked in wasn't subject to gossip?' he cut in sharply.

'Well, perhaps ... yes.' Gossip was hardly the word. When she had first begun going out with Kieron they had tried to keep their outings low-key, hoping not to inspire wagging tongues. And, though their affair had deepened, neither of them had wanted to broadcast their friendship lest people drew the wrong conclusions, which they had anyway despite all precautions.

'So I'll tell you now and get it over and done with.' His tone was curiously mechanical, a kind of blank look coming over his face. 'My wife and I ran a practice together near Truro. Sarah was a good vet – no ... I understate there; she was an exemplary vet.'

For a moment he paused, seeming to be lost in his own thoughts. 'We were working all the hours possible until Harry came along and then of course Sarah took time off with the baby until Audrey gave us a hand. Over the years we built up a good practice... Sarah threw herself into a heavy workload. During one bad winter the scale of emergencies was quite unprecedented...'

Gina studied his face as he talked. It was a strong, well-defined face, but devoid of expression, as though he was keeping all the emotion well behind the shuttered grey eyes.

'She went on a call from a farmer whose livestock had been caught in snow-drifts. She should never have chanced it, of course ... the winds were gale-force.' He shrugged, turning momentarily to the window, and Gina caught her breath at the pain she sensed behind the efficiently delivered explanation. When he looked at her again, she saw the mask of the professional back in place. 'A pylon came down in a field. Sarah didn't stand a chance; she was right underneath ... couldn't have known anything about it.'

Gina parted her lips on a silent gasp.

'Harry is fifteen now,' he went on unemotionally. 'Eighteen months ago Audrey decided she would like to return home to friends and family. We both miss her, but she had her own life to get on with – as we have ours. We decided, before Harry started examinations, we would make the break. Not an irrevocable one, I hasten to add, since Harry goes to stay with her grandmother during the holidays and I get down there when I can find the time.'

Gina asked, 'Does your daughter want to be a vet too?'

'Not at all!' His retort was sharp. 'Harry has no affinity with animals.' He turned away, slowly walking towards the porch. 'I think we've seen all we came to see, don't you? Shall we go back to the practice?' He brought out the keys from his pocket, indicating that the conversation was over.

Wishing she had never broached the subject of either wife or daughter, she asked expediently, 'I take it I'm being offered the job – formally, Mr Cassell?'

'Indeed you are. I've reservations as to whether I'm doing what is best – for both of us. But from my own point of view time is very relevant. Stuart can't possibly struggle on the way he has in surgery lately and Julian is far too busy at the branch practice at Rowhams to keep filling in here.'

Goodness, this man took some believing, Gina thought dazedly. He made it sound as if he had no choice other than to hire her! But, despite his attitude, he nevertheless was offering her the chance she needed to get back on her feet. And, all things considered, perhaps this was the challenge she was looking for.

'Thank you,' Gina said, her violet eyes brightening perceptibly. 'I'd very much like to have another look at the practice.'

He gestured to the front door and she

walked past him, lowering her head, sensing him move behind her. At the latch, she put out her hand and felt her skin tingle as, by mistake, he leaned across and covered her hand momentarily with his own.

'I'm sorry,' he muttered curtly. 'Just give the latch a sharp twist; sometimes it sticks.'

Removing her fingers and allowing him to jerk open the door, Gina found herself suddenly noting the deeply weather-hewn skin, its texture smooth yet intensely male, contrasting against the coppery pelt of hair. Sharply she thrust the faint stirrings of awareness out of her thoughts. Far too bound up with the memory of his wife to pose any emotional threat, Ben Cassell generated his own special brand of cool indifference, which, after Kieron, must surely be an added incentive to take this kind of post. No distractions, no emotional conflict, no intimate relationships ... just her career ... that was what she had promised herself. And, by the looks of it, that was exactly what she would have here at the Cassell Veterinary Clinic.

She heard the door clunk behind them.

'Incidentally ... how soon would you want me to start?' she asked, her delicate eyebrows pleated in a frown, her voice, for some reason, not quite steady as they walked the path.

'Monday wouldn't be too soon for us,

CORK CITY LIBRARIES

actually. It's a busy day this week.'

'Monday!' She thought about her parents and breaking the news to them – not that they would be unhappy, quite the reverse. They'd shared her frustration over the past months and would be relieved for her. Then what was holding her back? Perhaps just the final commitment, the final step back into reality.

'Does Monday pose a problem? Any domestic arrangements to be considered ... social engagements?'

'No...'

'Then Monday it is.'

And, once Gina had nodded her agreement, in the last of the afternoon sun they walked silently back together, with Gina uncomfortably aware of the powerful, brooding presence striding beside her ... and, even more disturbingly, of how her pulses had raced back there in the house when, for a brief few seconds, his fingers had covered hers.

CHAPTER TWO

On the Monday, unexpectedly, it snowed.

Gina left her parents' house, hidden below the gentle climb which led tourists in summer to the heart of the Purbecks, with two bulky suitcases loaded into the hatchback.

She switched on the wipers, thinking with amusement of her mother's reaction when she'd explained she would be moving into an annexe adjoining Ben Cassell's cottage. A delicate frown across her mother's forehead had said far more than words.

'There are no adjoining doors, Mother!' Gina had laughed lightly. 'It's completely self-contained, a pretty little flat built originally for Ben's mother-in-law, so the poor man has no devious motives for installing me there, I can assure you.'

Her father had added his own support. 'Gina's twenty-six, Marian, so stop fussing!'

Marian Travers had nevertheless expressed her continuing concern over the Sunday lunch. 'What if the job doesn't turn out to be suitable? Moving in right next door to the place–'

'Will make no difference at all as I'm only on a three month trial basis,' Gina had interrupted, smiling ruefully. 'I could endure anything for that small amount of time even if I had to work seven days a week–' And, realising her mistake as her mother's frown deepened, she had corrected herself sharply. 'Which I won't, because there's a rota system, of course, giving us all plenty of free time.'

Catching her father's wry, supportive grin, she'd reflected how good it was to have him on her side ... no battles now, like the earlier years. They had come a long way along the road to understanding one another...

Her farewells having gone smoothly, only one hurdle remained – becoming acquainted with the staff and the routine. A thrill of excitement passed through her as she thought of the fresh start ... she would make this job work, whatever it took!

Later, on a carpet of snow, she turned the Fiesta into the now familiar lane of poplars. Cases unloaded, glimpsing a few cars frosted in white already parked in the car park, Ben's Discovery among them, she wondered fleetingly if he would come to meet her.

Quite alone, though, she let herself in with the key he had given her, glancing at her watch ... a quarter to nine. No Ben, but then, she was rather early.

Leaving her cases in the bedroom, she strolled into the kitchen. In the silence all her perceptions seemed sharpened – the whiteness of the snow on the pocket lawn outside, the distinctive aroma of the flat like nutmeg and incense and the breathing of the place – a creaking floorboard, a gurgle of water through the pipes...

'Aga, microwave, dishwasher, split-level cooker, waste disposal ... hmm,' Gina murmured as she ran her fingers over the equipment in the kitchen, trying to form a picture in her mind of Audrey Farringdon. The tragedy of her daughter's death must have devastated her and yet, somehow, she had picked up the threads of life and cared for her granddaughter, Harriet, even to moving here with Ben, far from all her friends and the places which must have held so many memories.

Gina sighed, peering out of the window again. The countryside was swathed in snow, petal-sized drops falling from the sky, covering Audrey's shrubs and rambling roses. Coming into this place felt oddly like trying on another person's pair of comfortable slippers.

Turning her mind deliberately back to work, Gina found herself unable to restrain her enthusiasm to start. She threw on her hooded coat and stepped out on to the dazzling white path leading from her doorstep, along the narrow path of the front garden and onwards to the practice.

She had barely arrived halfway when the

cottage door jerked open to reveal Ben's tall figure. 'Morning!' he shouted, the phone cradled between head and shoulder as he beckoned her in through the wicket gate.

'But how in heaven's name did the pony get in there?' she heard him thunder as she stepped warily into the hall. A grandfather clock struck, melodiously requiring the caller to have to repeat himself and Ben to mutter darkly, 'Gorging itself on grain at this time of the year? You'll have to secure that store house, Frank. How many times have I warned you?'

Who was the unlucky caller? Gina wondered as she stood, wishing she was not witness to the altercation, noting the pen fly over the pad with more than a little annoyance.

'Frank Tavy,' Ben enlightened her as he rung off, harpooning the pen into its holder on the refectory table. 'His pony's nuzzled her way into his grain store and gorged herself. I'll have to get over there. He's worried she has abdominal pain. I can't for the life of me understand this man. Putting a padlock on the place would cost him no more time than ... oh ... I'm sorry...' He ran a large hand through the coppery hair. 'I should have welcomed you, but I didn't expect you this early.'

'I'm an early riser, I'm afraid. There didn't seem to be much point in waiting around after breakfast.' She watched the long, muscular limbs organise themselves into a waxed jacket and boots hurriedly. 'There's quite a heavy fall of snow in the Purbecks, so I thought I'd–'

'Try to make the right impression?' Grey eyes mockingly stared up at her.

She frowned. 'No ... that hadn't occurred to me...'

'But I told you to take your time! No sense in breaking your neck to get here, especially in weather conditions like this. As it happens, Stuart will be very pleased to see you, I expect,' he added condescendingly.

I'm glad there is someone who will, Gina reflected silently, wondering if her employer was always so abrasive first thing in the morning.

He straightened up, tearing the sheet of paper on which he had written from the pad and thrusting it into his coat pocket. 'What about your unpacking?' he queried shortly.

'I've not an enormous amount with me, just a couple of suitcases. I'll pick up anything else I need later.'

He gave her another doubtful look. 'And the annexe, is it warm enough?' Glancing at his wristwatch, he sighed impatiently without waiting for an answer. 'The snow will make the going harder – roads around here are abysmal when there's a change in the weather.' And, halfway to the door, he turned back as though just remembering she was there. 'Oh, we've a cleaner who comes in part-time here to the cottage. Mrs Swain. She's quite reliable. You can leave messages with her if Harry's not about.'

A vague smile touched his lips as he snatched his case and trod out into the snow. Following on his heel, Gina only just managed to pull up sharply as he swung around again.

'Where do you think you're off to?' he asked, a deep frown pleating his forehead.

'I'm going with you ... to the practice. Won't you be introducing me?'

'Heavens above ... I haven't time for introductions! No doubt you'll find your way around easily enough. The girls will steer you in the right direction.'

'But I–'

'And anyway, you'd better make yourself known to Harry first... Harry! Miss Travers has arrived. A quick cup of coffee wouldn't go amiss!' he shouted back into the house.

Then as Ben nodded briskly and hurried off down the path, Gina found herself watching the disappearing figure. Feeling somewhat abandoned, she hesitated. No one appeared from the interior of the house. She was tempted just to close the door and proceed across to the practice as she saw the Land Rover Discovery glide out of the car park, Ben hunched over the wheel. But curiosity drove her back into the warmth and she gave the door a firm push to in the hopes it might evoke a response from the silent Harry.

The house remained eerily quiet ... only the rhythmic ticking of the grandfather clock and, from somewhere, the faint sound of music.

'Well, it's been nice meeting you, too,' she muttered, staring at the blank space which a few moments ago had generated the large figure of Ben Cassell.

She waited, but Harry didn't appear. It would seem unfriendly, though, if she didn't introduce herself and yet if Ben's daughter could not – or would not – appear, should she really trespass further into the house?

Her problem was solved when a furry body wrapped itself around her legs in the form of a black cat with huge green eyes. Its miaow resonated with a deep purr and Gina bent down to stroke it. Prepared for a show of playful claws, the cat surprised her by rubbing its nose on her shoes and walking ahead, as if showing her the way.

'I hope you're not leading me astray, puss,' Gina warned the erect tail. The music grew louder as she followed down the hallway and the cat sedately ignored all connecting rooms, finally stopping at a frosted-glass door.

'We're here, are we? OK, you go first and make the introductions.' Gina helped the door on its way and stared into a huge kitchen, its walls fitted with rows of mahogany cupboards.

Harry, she supposed, stood with her back to her. A slight figure with cropped fair hair, wearing a long navy school-skirt and baggy cardigan, propped at the sink, her sleeves pushed up.

'Hi there! Harry?' Gina called.

The cat jumped up on the worktop, to be swished with a cloth. 'Get down, Tabitha!' Briskly shooed from her perch, Tabitha bolted for a saucer of milk. 'My name's Harriet, actually,' said the girl with no more than a brief glance over her shoulder.

'Oh, I'm sorry – Harriet. I'm – er – Gina Travers ... and I just–'

'I know who you are,' came the uninterested reply. 'Daddy told me. Do you want a coffee?'

So Harriet had heard her father call, but had no intention of making an appearance. 'No ... no, thanks. I can see you're busy. I just thought I'd say hello before I dive in next door. Tabitha showed me the way to the kitchen.'

She was caught by the slope of the shoulders, the air of gloom surrounding Harriet. Something tugged at her heart despite the vibes of antipathy. Many years ago she could remember standing at a sink wishing her frustrated adolescence would run down the drain with the bubbles, too. It was probably best to leave her alone and Gina was about to make herself scarce when Harriet turned slowly.

'Tabitha's a nuisance!' Harriet glowered at the cat. 'We inherited her when we moved here ... cats are too independent for my liking.' She stared at Gina, pausing to wipe her hands on a cloth. 'In fact, I don't like animals much at all.'

Gina nodded. 'They can be an enormous responsibility – something a lot of people don't consider when they buy a pup for Christmas, not realising it's for life.'

Harriet chewed on her bottom lip, looking as though she was trying to find another equally dramatic statement to make.

'I suppose I had better hurry along.' Gina smiled. 'To be frank, I've a few butterflies about meeting everyone.'

Harriet Cassell looked surprised. 'You needn't have. Stuart's really nice and the nurses are too.' The girl perched herself on the edge of the kitchen table, swinging her legs. Bar the usual cluster of adolescent spots and disregarding the earlier pout, Gina could see just what an attractive girl she was and, with a sudden start, had the feeling she was looking into the mirror-image of Sarah Cassell. The pale, adolescent beauty, the heart-shaped face, the dainty features were nothing like Ben's tough profile ... this must be Sarah. She must have been a remarkably beautiful woman…

When the phone rang Gina jumped, lost in thought, a strange little ache lingering at her ribs as she tried to dismiss the overwhelming presence of Ben's wife from her mind.

Harriet's face darkened as she picked up the telephone with a curt, 'Yes?'

The conversation was ice-cool and brief. 'They always want Daddy,' Harriet grumbled when she had finished. 'It's never enough that he's in surgery all hours, they always have to phone up here. Anyway, that was only Vivienne Armitage. I expect you'll meet her soon. She's always phoning or calling for something or other. You'd think Daddy was at her personal beck and call!'

Gina absorbed this in silence. Obviously the lady was not a favourite with Harriet.

Harriet sighed. 'I'd better go. I'm late for the bus this morning. It's just lucky we had a free period to start with.'

Gina smiled, moving towards the door past a purring Tabitha. 'Come over and have a coffee with me some time. You can tell me what flowers your grandmother liked to grow.'

The response was hardly reassuring. Harriet frowned under her disorderly cap of fair hair. Now, that was Ben, Gina decided wryly. It was strange how the resemblance was so noticeable, more in an expression than in anything else.

Gina reflectively left the cottage and made her way across to the practice. The lights shone out welcomingly into the grey morning and she found Reception warm and cosy as she walked in, a couple of dog owners ensconced by the window, deep in conversation.

'You must be Gina?' A brown-haired girl in a green nurse's uniform looked up from the computer on the desk. She had an instant and friendly smile and signalled Gina to come across. 'I'm Bev. Vicki – the head nurse – is in with Stuart; she'll be out in a minute. How have you settled in?'

'Fine, thanks, Bev... I've hardly had time to get my bearings, but ... yes, so far so good. Actually, I've just introduced myself to Harriet.'

'Oh!' Bev nodded slowly. 'You'll get to like Harry as you know her more; she's just a bit lonely, I think. It's a pity she couldn't come and give us a hand over here in her spare time. I think she'd really end up liking it.'

Before Bev could enlarge, Gina stepped back, allowing a dog on a lead to pass with its owner. Why, she wondered, didn't Harriet help out in her father's practice? She could hardly believe the girl's dislike of animals was so great that she wouldn't venture in on the odd occasion. But she had no more time to mull the puzzle over as she watched Bev hurriedly separate a pair of quarrelsome terriers.

The room was filling up, she noticed, as a hyperactive Weimaraner jerked its owner into the hall and two more people came in despite the weather conditions outside.

'You're busy!' Gina grinned and Bev nodded, tapping in the details of the last patient on the keyboard. 'The snow doesn't seem to have put people off, does it?'

Bev raised her eyes to the ceiling. 'Some hopes! Go into Stuart now before the next one, Gina. Two doors along on the right. He's going to shout hallelujah when he sees you!'

Gina made her way along to the consulting-room, passing a client on the way. Both Stuart Roberts and the head nurse, Vicki, smiled as she walked in and introduced herself. Vicki, a tall girl with dark hair swept into a ponytail, hurried off to Reception, explaining that when they had five minutes she would show Gina where everything was kept.

'Brilliant!' gasped Stuart Roberts. 'You've made my day, I can tell you. Look at the list!' Lean and lanky with fair hair and roaming blue eyes, the young vet pushed a spectacularly crumpled piece of paper into her hand. 'My God, you're beautiful! Are you sure you're our new locum – or am I hallucinating?'

Gina laughed, her long jet hair framing her oval face as she flushed under his teasing flattery – and the overwhelming relief that the ice had been broken. As for Ben ... she tried not to think too much about him, turning her mind from their initial brief and disappointingly brusque encounter.

Soon Stuart had installed her in the consulting-room next door. 'Thrown in at the deep end,' he observed with a disarming smile leaving her awaiting her first client in two years.

Vicki provided her with a new white coat, nodding approvingly at Gina's slender outline. 'Great! You'll do! Now I must speak to you about Archie; he's diabetic and–'

Mrs Forbuoys entered of her own accord and hoisted a disgruntled Archie on to the bench. He snarled, bristling with typical Jack Russell indignation. 'I don't know what's come over him! He's taken a dislike to me giving him his insulin.'

Gina smoothed down the rough coat as the rumbling died down. 'When did this start, Mrs Forbuoys?'

The lady guiltily eyed her pet. 'I had to leave him for a couple of weeks and someone else did the injections. When I came back – well, perhaps he's just sulking ... but he turns on me, and he never has before.'

Gina read Archie's notes, recognising the scrawl which was Ben's, identical to the writing she had seen on the pad in the cottage. 'Perhaps if we could get his confidence back? Maybe try a bribe and give him a special treat so he'll associate the injection with something pleasurable. Vicki, do we have something we could offer?'

The nurse hurried out of the room and came back with a small dish of chopped tinned meat. Archie sniffed the air with terrier enthusiasm.

'Since only a very small quantity of insulin is necessary,' she explained carefully, 'we administer with a fine-bore needle. I can reassure you that Archie feels very little discomfort, so it's not actually the injection itself which is worrying him. What has probably happened is he associates being left with the giving of his insulin. All we have to do now is counteract the fear into pleasure. Vicki, just show him the treat, will you? Perhaps give him a tablespoonful so he knows something good is on its way.'

Vickie fed Archie a little, then a little more. The black eyes darted greedily back to the dish. 'Now, Mrs Forbuoys, I'll administer the insulin if you will offer him the rest of the food.'

Archie needed no encouragement.

As he nibbled eagerly, Vicki sterilised the area on his neck with one or two deft strokes and Gina held the fold of skin between her ·
thumb and forefinger, inserting the needle, keeping the syringe parallel to the fold but with the needle angled downwards. Depress-

ing the plunger, Archie barely noticed what was going on.

After he'd gulped down his last tit-bit Archie's tail gave an electric wag of satisfaction.

'He didn't even notice!' Mrs Forbuoys sighed with relief.

'It's a wonder what a little bribery will do.' Gina grinned. 'He's quite happy with life now, and my guess is you won't have any trouble if you repeat this procedure a few times.'

'Thank you ... Miss...?'

'Gina. Gina Travers. I'm Mr Cassell's locum. Feel free to call me any time if you're worried.'

As Mrs Forbuoys left with Archie, Gina decided she had been apprehensive about her first morning for nothing. Jumping in at the deep end, as Stuart had so aptly put it, had been the perfect way of getting back into the swing ... that was, until the door opened and Ben appeared.

'Is anything wrong?' she asked in surprise.

He shook his head, standing quite still in his top coat, obviously not about to stay, but indecisive enough to put her on edge.

'Did you see the pony?' she asked, hoping the next client would be brought in and she could get on with her work.

'No ... I had to come back for some drugs I thought I might need – I'm just going into the dispensary... Was that Mrs Forbuoys I saw going out?'

'Yes, with Archie.' She frowned at him. 'Is there something I ought to know?'

Ben shrugged. 'No ... no. If you managed...'

And, as once before this morning, he disappeared, leaving her curiously unsettled.

Unwilling to allow herself to dwell on his attitude, Gina examined a small green cagebird brought in by an elderly client. The sadly emaciated breastbone under her fingers indicated a very sick little creature. Discovering a tumour on the reproductive organs, she was unable to offer treatment and, knowing how much even a budgerigar could mean to a person living on their own, after putting him out of his pain, Gina sat awhile with the lady and talked to her as she recovered.

Vicki and Bev dived for the coffee-pot at lunchtime in the staffroom. Gina sat with the nurses, talking over the assortment of cases she'd seen: routine vaccinations, a rabbit with an abscess which she had drained and treated and an old retriever who was experiencing spasmodic urinary incontinence. Although the dog was elderly and the problem was due to the loss of function of the nerves controlling the bladder, at least with drug therapy she could help for the time being.

The morning, she decided, apart from Ben's interruption, had been successful on the whole. She hadn't had to ask Stuart for help and the nurses she found efficient and helpful. Both were in their early twenties and devoted to animals, and now she listened with amusement to their conversation.

'Julian, who you have yet to meet, is dishy for an older man.' Bev sighed. 'But he's married with three children and he's dedicated to his work – unfortunately!'

'And Stuart's a wolf in sheep's clothing … a wolf with a reputation to match!' Vicki added teasingly. 'We still fancy him, though, but he never mixes business with pleasure!'

Sensible man, Gina decided, recollecting her heartache over Kieron Brent. For a moment, she was back in the go-ahead Surrey practice she had worked in on her last year qualifying, where she had met Kieron, the junior partner of the firm. Blond, tall and amazingly attentive, he had swept her off her feet. Nothing had prepared her for the way first love sent everything else by the board; even her career had become less focused.

Not that Kieron had felt the same way about her, she reflected grimly, nor had ever pretended he was anything else but a confirmed bachelor. But when the firm had offered her a post after qualifying she had hoped, so desperately hoped, that their relationship had begun to mean something more to him. Was it the car accident which had ended their affair? she had wondered time and again. Or was it that the brutal truth had been driven home in a way that made her see the facts for what they really were? That Kieron just didn't want the responsibility of a wife, much less the embarrassment of a virtual cripple in his life?

Immediately annoyed with herself for allowing her thoughts to wander, she was relieved to hear whistling and the approach of footsteps.

'Talking about me? Is it something sexy and devious?' Stuart asked, strolling casually in.

'See what we mean?' Vicki laughed.

Stuart grimaced. 'I'll catch you later in private, Gina. You can tell me exactly what they've been saying!' With this, everyone burst into laughter, prompting Gina to decide that she would have no problem at all with the easy going staff, even a rather dour Julian who called later in the afternoon.

'Good to have you with us, Gina,' he welcomed her soberly and, after a few minutes' friendly conversation, left to return to the branch practice at Rowhams.

At the close of the afternoon Gina met with only one set back – the last client, who refused to be seen by a locum. Suturing the two-inch-long wound on the Great Dane's back incurred in a dog fight would have taken her no time at all. The owner, however, disgruntled by the fact that a woman had owned the attacking dog and had refused to restrain her dog on a lead, projected his irritation on to Gina.

After Stuart had treated the dog, she walked into his room with a crestfallen expression but he simply laughed.

'Don't for one minute let that little display of prejudice worry you, Gina! It was unfortunate on your first day ... but you'll be ready next time and it won't matter so much, not when you've a few weeks of practice under your belt.'

Stripping off his white coat, he revealed a white shirt embroidered by hundreds of tiny creases. 'I hate ironing,' he apologised, catching her gaze as he hurriedly slipped on a sports jacket. 'My current girlfriend has never used an iron, as far as I can gather!'

'Then you'll have to train her a little better.' She smiled easily, grateful for his humour.

'Oh, no! Dogs, horses, yes ... they'll train. But women, no! Delicious creatures, but a law until themselves!'

Stuart glanced at himself in the wall mirror, straightening his tie and at the same time flicking his gaze to her. 'Ben only told me in brief ... about your accident, Gina. He said it would save you time having to explain.'

'He's very efficient,' she murmured coolly.

Stuart turned. 'Oh, you'll get used to him; his growl means nothing. He's had a difficult time over the last few years ... but enough about us! I want to hear about you … a beautiful single woman in our midst, a mystery woman, with a deep, dark secret perhaps?' he suggested with such teasing flattery that she wasn't offended.

'Another day, maybe,' she compromised, suddenly feeling the tiredness creep over her. 'I think I'll just enter a few more notes for my own benefit before I leave tonight.'

'Good lord, such enthusiasm! Ben didn't know how lucky he was when Gerald Gorley dropped out at the last minute.'

Gina's smile faded as she shook her head. 'Sorry? Gerald Gorley?'

'Oh, dear!' Stuart frowned and scratched his chin nervously. 'I've put both feet in it now, haven't I? I thought Ben would have told you.'

'Someone else was supposed to start, you mean?'

He nodded. 'This Gorley chap let us down at the last minute. Can't say I'm sorry, though. Hey, forget it. It doesn't matter. If Ben had interviewed you first he would have snapped you up.'

Gina doubted that. Ben Cassell had conveniently omitted the fact that someone else had been due to begin here. Was he so desperate that he had hired her as a last resort? She'd hoped – well, that was silly too – she'd struck a chord with him, but now she wondered if his attitude wasn't due to the fact that he had been put on the spot and been forced to engage a locum he felt unsuitable.

Leaving Stuart, Gina went into the office to familiarise herself with some of the records. In the morning, she told herself sternly, the fact that Ben had hired her as a poor substitute would seem far less important.

On her own, she became engrossed in some of the cases and it wasn't until much later that she heard the front door unlock.

'Not still here, surely?' Ben looked in at her, frowning.

She smiled, getting up to stretch her back. 'Catching up on a few notes, that's all. I didn't realise how much–'

'You're not expected to work overtime.' He stood with his wax coat dripping wet and his face tense.

'I … I didn't think of it as overtime. I was just interested in some of the cases.'

'Even so … you shouldn't be here at this hour.'

Trying to avoid his cool stare, she enquired politely, 'How was Frank Tavy's pony this morning?'

'False alarm. The abdominal pain had worn off by the time I got there. He'd been walking her off her feet so she wouldn't roll and twist her bowel.' His frown deepened as his gaze slid down to the file in her hands. 'What have you got there?'

She flipped it open. 'I've made a few notes over the day; I wondered if we could briefly run over them?'

He shook his head. 'I'm sorry, but my day is over.'

She could hardly believe his attitude! Her notes would take no more than five minutes to review. Maybe she was a little over-enthusiastic, but was that to be so sharply discouraged? Seeing there was no point in arguing, reluctantly she complied, replacing the file. In silence, as he waited for her, she gathered her coat and bag and switched off the light.

'You aren't expected to work yourself into the ground,' he said as they reached Reception – as though she would forget the fact! 'This place isn't your responsibility, it's mine. I would appreciate it if you remembered that. And one thing more... Mrs Forbuoys ... how did you come to see her? I ask because Vicki usually books her in with me.'

Gina stopped, her heart thudding, trying to beat back the sensation that she was having to defend herself from every corner.

'I ... I think probably Mrs Forbuoys was in a panic with Archie. She had been away and he seemed to resent her giving him the insulin on her return and because he is diabetic–'

'I'm perfectly aware Archie is diabetic,' he cut in brusquely. 'But we do usually try to see our own patients when possible. Anyway, no point in making a harangue about it now; it's been a long day.'

'But I'd rather clear this point with you…' Gina began, only to be stopped by the sound of the phone ringing in the office.

'I'll get it.' He marched off, leaving her staring after him in frustration. And when, some minutes later, Ben hadn't returned, she decided to wait no longer. She must speak to him … it would be no use trying to rest this evening if she couldn't put the misunderstanding straight. But when she arrived at the office he was seated, smiling casually as he talked on the telephone.

He looked up. 'It's for me. Personal,' he said, cupping the mouthpiece with his hand. 'You go on and I'll lock up.'

She paused, meeting his gaze, finding herself locked in momentary challenge with the steel-grey eyes. 'But Ben, I must talk to you about–'

'Gina! I said – it's time you weren't here! Do I always have to repeat myself twice? Now please – go home!' There was such vehemence in his voice that she flinched visibly.

As she walked away, a tide of colour washed up from her neck to her face. She felt inarticulate with anger … and humiliation.

Surely, after her first day, Ben Cassell could apportion her some of his valuable time … or was this the precedent he had set for a locum he secretly scorned?

CHAPTER THREE

Despite Ben's warning, whenever the opportunity presented itself, Gina ensconced herself in the office with the records in order to
bring herself up to date with the case histories. She wanted to make no mistakes now.
It seemed even more vital that she should
prove herself to be capable of the work and
prove Ben wrong in his doubts about her.

Friday came with a sudden thaw and the
first glimmer of sunshine through grey skies.
Gina arrived in surgery well before eight,
intending to make coffee in the staffroom
and browse through the *Veterinary Record*
before anyone arrived.

A noise in the corridor made her look up,
her violet eyes widening in surprise at her
visitor. 'Harriet ... what a pleasant surprise
... come in!'

The girl moved into the office slowly.
'Hello, Gina.'

'Would you like some coffee with me?'

Harriet shook her head. She was dressed
for school, but carried no books or bag with
her. Gina had only glimpsed Harriet as she
walked to work each day and had waved,
but the girl hadn't taken her up on paying a

visit and Gina was beginning to wonder if Ben had dissuaded her.

'You're on your way to school?'

'Almost...' She looked guardedly under her lashes. 'I was going to call around this week, but I knew you were busy.'

'Not at all. I could have done with some company, as it happens.'

'Really?' Harriet's blue eyes were curious. 'I thought all vets were rushed off their feet?'

Gina grinned. 'I'm just the locum, remember.'

'Not "just". Daddy said you've taken over half the practice this week.'

'Oh, did he?' She could well imagine in what context he had meant that! 'I hope I've pulled my weight. It's been a bit nerve-racking but on the whole I've loved every minute. There haven't been too many sad cases, so I've been lucky.'

Since Harriet stood chewing on her lip, Gina was forced to put her own interpretation on the silence. 'Is ... is there something you would like to talk about, Harriet?'

'Well, yes ... what I mean is, I've got to catch the bus for school .. and I've got something to show you ... in the consulting-room next door.'

Surprised, Gina stood up. 'Sounds intriguing. Let's take a look, shall we?'

The noise was enough to reveal what was in the cardboard box on her treatment table. 'Kittens?' Gina frowned.

The girl nodded. 'Three of them. Little tabby ones.'

Gina folded back the top of the box and gave a surprised gasp. 'My goodness ... who do they belong to?'

'You'll never believe it, but I found them on the doorstep,' Harriet said, her face softening as she looked at them. 'I think whoever put them there must have thought we were the practice. Daddy had just left to go out on a emergency this morning ... it was about sixish ... and I though he was coming back for something he'd forgotten. I heard the garden gate go – and I opened the door and saw the box.'

Gina lifted one of the furry bodies and looked into its midnight-blue eyes. Then she examined the other two and watched as Harriet cupped the tiniest one in the palm of her hand.

'They're weaned,' Harriet suddenly said. 'I gave them some of Tabitha's food and they gobbled it up.'

Gina examined the soft, protruding bellies and nodded. 'I'd say they're about six to seven weeks old – and the small one you're holding is the only one who looks poorly. Perhaps their mother died or the owner couldn't look after them any more. At least they brought them to the right place and didn't leave them in the middle of a wood somewhere.'

Harriet wrapped the kitten in the opening of her cardigan and gently traced a finger over the ruffled tabby brow and miniature whiskers. 'I'm not very keen on animals normally,' she murmured. 'But I've been thinking … we could keep them in the kitchen with a litter tray for the time being. Mrs Swain could keep an eye on them while I'm at school.'

Gina smiled, nodding slowly. 'Yes … I suppose so. But you would have to ask your father first. They will need their vaccinations; that's most important. Cats play host to several parasites too. Fleas among other things. You see … along here…?'

Gina folded back the hairs on the head of one of the kittens and brushed them down along the backbone. 'These are the common places. And roundworms can be passed on to kittens via their mother's milk, too. Perhaps that's what's wrong with the little one. The worms feed on partly digested food in the kitten's digestive tract.'

'Does it hurt them inside?' Harriet curled her finger between a pair of tiny paws, frowning.

'No, but it's uncomfortable. But in a few days we should have them well. When Vicki or Bev comes in, they can have another small feed and then go into a warm recovery cage. Then perhaps … you could talk with your father about looking after them.'

Harriet's face darkened as she lowered the kitten back to the box. 'Do they miss their mother, do you think?'

Gina felt a pang of sympathy for the girl. She was only nine when her mother died ... no wonder she felt she could relate to these orphaned kittens. 'This has probably been an unsettling experience for them ... being shut up in a box, taken out of their surroundings and left on a cold doorstep. Moreover, they come into a strange-smelling surgery, are prodded around by people they don't know... I think all they will want today is food, warmth, peace and quiet.'

'Who wants peace and quiet?' a deep voice behind them asked. They both swivelled around to see Ben standing in the doorway. He walked over and peered into the box, his dark eyebrows lifting as he saw the contents.

'Three little orphans, Daddy. I found them right on our doorstep after you left, mewing their heads off. So I took them in and warmed them up. They were really hungry too...'

'You don't know who left them?'

'Haven't an earthly, but Gina says they may have fleas and worms and so they'll have to stay here for a while but I thought ... well, you see Tabitha took an instant liking to them and I thought–'

'I suppose you realise you've missed your

bus?' Ben interrupted, frowning. 'You were late on Monday too.' He lifted one of the kittens. 'Pretty little thing…'

'What shall we do with them?' Harriet stared at her father.

Ben lowered the kitten gently back into the box. 'We'll cross that bridge when we come to it, young lady. Now go and collect your things for school and I'll run you in.'

Harriet grinned under her lashes at Gina as she left, leaving Gina to register Ben's scowl. 'Beats me how some people can abandon their animals,' he said with a sigh. 'They could have frozen on the doorstep.'

'Had not Harriet taken them in,' Gina observed.

He nodded, the grey eyes puzzled. 'She's taken a liking to them, hasn't she?'

Gina smiled and nodded, deciding she would not risk a plea on Harriet's part, though, by the expression of the grey eyes, the girl would have little trouble in convincing her father to adopt the kittens temporarily.

'Harriet said you had an emergency this morning?'

'Yes, a Caesar, a little mongrel bitch well overdue. She delivered two live puppies but the other, unfortunately, was dead.' He added distractedly, 'I'd better get a move on. Julian's off with a flu virus. Just the day I have a fair bit on, too.'

'Stuart and I have no appointments ... if he could handle open surgery...' she suggested warily.

The grey eyes travelled slowly over her face. This morning she had coiled her dark hair back and wound it into a plait, a dark wing softly falling across her forehead enhancing the ivory colouring of her clear skin. She wore a slim-fitting winter dress in angora wool, creamy and clinging, revealing her feminine curves and long legs.

'You're not dressed for farm work.' He grinned. 'But thanks anyway.'

She shrugged, encouraged by the smile which played around his mouth. 'Give me five minutes to change. By then the nurses and Stuart will have arrived. I'm sure he'll be quite happy to cover for me this morning.'

He stared at her and for a few moments she gazed hesitantly back at him. 'If you really do mean five minutes and not hours...' he sighed '...and if Stuart can manage... I suppose another pair of hands will come in useful.'

As she ran across to the flat, she passed Harriet, her school-bag slung across her shoulder. 'I'm coming with you,' Gina called. 'Your father needs help with a farm visit.'

'Super! See you in the Discovery,' Harriet returned.

And, with a strangely light heart, Gina

rushed in to change.

Harriet chatted non-stop.

Gins sat quietly in the passenger seat as Harriet leant forward from the rear, her elbows perched on the back of their seats. The topic, not surprisingly, was the kittens. Gina managed a sly look at Ben who was concentrating on the slushy roads, the snow rapidly disappearing except in the lanes where it lingered stubbornly in the hedge-rows.

Eventually they arrived, Harriet jumping out and peering in through Gina's open window. 'See you later ... and thanks for everything, Gina.'

They watched her run across the road to a waiting group of girls. 'St Mary's!' Gina gasped, suddenly realising where they were. 'My old school.'

'What a coincidence,' Ben remarked drily beside her.

'It's a lovely school,' Gina said with enthusiasm. 'I'm sure Harriet is happy here, isn't she?'

He shrugged. 'On the whole I'd say she is.' Then he added as he started the engine, 'You know, it's funny, but Harry is very selective about whom she likes and, mostly, whom she dislikes! But you seem to have made an impact... I wonder why?'

Gina hesitated. 'An impact?'

'I've never known her to show an interest in animals. All of a sudden she seems very enthusiastic.'

'Well, most kids love animals,' she answered defensively. 'I don't think Harriet's an exception.'

'Don't you?'

She glanced at him quickly, feeling he did not welcome her comments on his daughter. Sitting back in her seat with a sigh, she began to wonder if there was any topic on which she and Ben Cassell did agree!

'I find adolescence hard to deal with,' he said out of the blue and she turned to look at him again, surprised to find him quite serious. 'When she was younger, things were so much more straightforward. I suppose the generation gap is beginning to show. Thirty-six must be ancient in her book.'

She smiled at his self-mockery, drawn to the disarming honesty of his statement. 'You were probably exactly the same as Harriet at fifteen. Rebellion is all part of growing up, isn't it?'

'Oh?' He chuckled. 'Do I take it we have a frustrated anarchist in our midst?'

She laughed at this. Once it might have been true of her, but not now. 'I thought I knew what I wanted at fifteen and I just couldn't get it across to my parents. But I've never regretted becoming a vet. I just wish I'd had brothers or sisters who might have gone into the family business for my parents' sake.'

'I'm sure they coped without you,' he commented wryly as the vehicle gathered speed. 'Your happiness is what they wanted, as I have Harry's happiness at heart.'

'Sometimes that's hard to get through to an adolescent.' She sighed.

'My point exactly. I've only one reason for wanting her to pursue her science subjects and that's because she's very good at them ... naturally good. With A levels she would have a choice to do whatever she really liked with her future. It's just that she doesn't talk much about what she really wants from life.'

'Did you know what you wanted at fifteen?' Gina ventured with care.

He grinned broadly. 'As a matter of fact, yes. Father was a marine biologist and we travelled constantly with him, quite a bit to the States, where Marcus, my brother, settled eventually. Perhaps it was because we had too much movement in our lives that we both decided roaming around the planet was the last thing we wanted to do. But I think I always wanted to be a vet ... from a very early age.'

'What made you choose Cornwall?' she asked curiously.

'My parents died while I was at university. Father went first and I don't think there was anything to keep Mother here after that. Then I met Sarah. She came from Truro ...

it was as good a place as any to put up our plates after we'd qualified.'

Gina noticed the rigid control in the face, a small muscle working in his jaw as he talked of his wife. She listened with a kind of hollow sensation in her stomach, leaving her feeling bewildered and confused. Why should she react this way when they talked about Sarah? Why, come to that, was she so edgy when confronted with Sarah's lingering presence in the Cassell household ... even in Ben's words ... stirring up a strange anguish inside her?

She drew a long, deep breath. 'Girls often change most during adolescence,' she commented, steering the conversation towards Harriet again. 'Look at how she took to those kittens this morning.'

'But why come to you?' Ben pointed out reasonably. 'Why not wait for me to get back?'

Gina found herself apprehensively considering the question, Harriet's actions certainly seeming to suggest deliberate thought ... possibly trying to gain her father's attention?

'I'm sure that's reading too much into it.' She smiled and felt relief as he nodded, giving a shrug.

At last the Armitage farm emerged from the mists, and Ben gestured to a rambling country house set back among trees. 'This place belongs to a friend of mine, Viv Armitage. Reggie Armitage, Viv's husband, ran it until a few years back. But there were domestic problems and eventually a divorce. Viv retained the farm and Reggie went overseas. She decided to employ a manager after that. Harvey Green's not a bad chap, a bit long in the tooth, but very reliable. He's had no trouble with the herd until this morning. One of his milkers has gone down in the milking yard.'

Gina refrained from saying what she already knew of the lady from Harriet and the snippets of gossip she had overheard in the staffroom. It was almost impossible on occasions not to hear, Vicki and Bev being no exception to the grapevine rule.

As they drove past the house and into the yard, a harassed-looking man in a cloth-cap hurried from the dairy, signalling them to where the cow lay, just as Harvey had explained.

'I've cleaned her up and milked her where she is.' Harvey had washed the debris away with the hose and a broom, keeping the area meticulously clean.

'She won't even try to get up?' Ben queried.

Harvey shook his head. 'We've tried everything.'

Ben got down on his haunches and examined the udder. Gina reflected that, by definition, mastitis was an inflammation of the mammary gland and about a quarter of the udder certainly looked inflamed, though it was impossible to get a good look underneath it, but the longer she lay here, the greater the chance of it becoming infected.

'Did you notice if she damaged the teats as she fell or was the inflammation there before?' Ben asked.

Harvey frowned. 'As far as I know she was clean as a whistle yesterday.'

Ben looked puzzled. 'Mastitis can be responsible for recumbency … but I'm not so sure in this case. Is she eating?'

'Hasn't stopped.'

'Perhaps she has downer cow syndrome,' Gina suggested, thinking of the perplexing and often unrewarding condition when nothing specific could be found to be wrong or the initial problem having receded, the animal stubbornly decided to stay put. 'Her teats aren't normal by any means but they aren't badly infected either,' Gina persevered as the two men stared at her. 'She just may have made up her mind not to move.'

Ben gave the cow another quick inspection, then, as he rose, frowned apologetically. 'Oh, Harvey, I'm sorry; I should have introduced you … this is our new locum, Gina Travers.'

Gina smiled at the non-committal Harvey, eliciting a nod as a response. 'A half-ton cow like this will soon have pressure sores on concrete,' she said thoughtfully, 'then she'll lose all her confidence to get up. It would be better if we could get her on to fresh straw under cover, don't you think?'

'Naturally,' Harvey agreed sharply. 'But you just try moving her. I was hoping you'd give her an injection or something to get her off her rump.'

'I'd give my right arm for a drug that would,' Ben responded dully.

'That gate would do.' Gina nodded towards a pile of disused equipment. 'If we had some manpower to roll her over on to it.'

Ben looked around. 'Harvey, have you got the tractor handy?'

'I can get it here.'

'And a shed where we can put her on a deep bed of straw?'

'Bags of space, but are we going to tow her there?'

'We're going to have a damn good try,' Ben assured him and, smiling at Gina, he began to take off his coat. When she did the same, revealing a slim figure in overalls, he shook his head. 'You're not attempting any physical work, Gina … so don't even think about it. And I don't want an argument this time.'

'But I could help!' Gina moved, but he grabbed her arm.

'No! Leave it to us.'

'I'll fetch the lads!' Harvey intervened, frowning at them, and she was forced to watch as Ben went over to the gate and began hauling it out from the scrap-metal pile. She was perfectly fit now, but persuading Ben Cassell of that fact seemed impossible!

Soon the farm-hands arrived and began tugging the gate to where the cow lay. Ignominiously she was rolled on to it and the gate hitched to the tractor. Harvey made a thumbs-up sign from the cab and Gina watched the ensemble move off, dismally aware that she had been of no use at all.

'Miss Travers?' Startled, Gina turned to find a woman standing behind her, her attention focused on the figure of Ben, his brown forearms flexed and gleaming in the cold as he wrestled with the other men to keep the gate on course. 'I'm Vivienne Armitage.'

Gina smiled and held out her hand, taking in the woman's elegant style of dress and ash-blonde hair fashionably curled into a bob. Though possibly in her thirties, she looked very much younger, with clear, observant hazel eyes.

'How is the cow?' she asked uninterestedly.

'The men are moving her under-cover. We're not sure it's mastitis ... she may simply be stubborn about getting up.'

'Really? Is that Ben's diagnosis or yours?'

Gina hesitated. 'Perhaps you had better ask Ben yourself,' she countered calmly.

'Perhaps I will. I thought you were brought in to help out with the surgery work. Surely farm animals aren't your cup of tea?'

'On the contrary,' Gina demurred, unwilling to be ruffled. 'I'm trained – as every vet is – as an all-rounder, but as Ben's short on small-animal assistants at the moment I'm helping in surgery.'

'How fortunate Ben is!' The eyes assessed her again, more carefully this time. 'And how long have you known him?'

Gina had already noticed the slim, ringless finger, aware that Vivienne was far more interested in Ben Cassell in a personal sense than in his professional capacity as a vet. Was she the person who'd been speaking to him on the telephone the other night? Vivienne Armitage seemed to know an awful lot about her, information which only Ben could have divulged. 'Not long,' Gina answered efficiently.

'You seem to be finding your feet remarkably well, Gina. I may call you Gina, may I?' The question was obviously rhetorical as she quickly added, 'I'm glad we met. I enjoy meeting all Ben's friends. I'm sure our paths will cross again.'

No doubt of that, thought Gina as she watched the fashionable heels side-stepping the puddles back to the house. So Vicki and Bev, in this case, had not been so far from the truth when they had speculated on the romance between the handsome vet and his attractive client!

Gina hurried on to catch up with the others, her mind racing. Had she just received a warning to steer clear from Ben? But Vivienne Armitage had no cause to worry. Ben was the last man on earth she would consider becoming involved with and he hadn't the remotest interest in her. She had learnt a big lesson from her experience with Kieron: flirtations were one thing, like those of Stuart and the girls, light-hearted fun and teasing – even occasional dates among the staff members. But anything more serious only led to heartache as far as she was concerned, a heartache she had no wish to repeat ever again.

Her arrival in the doorway of the shed caused little reaction. The men, having successfully transported the cow to her destination, were engrossed in theoretically diagnosing her condition. She looked as comfortable as a queen, lying on her bed of straw, and the more Gina studied her, the more she felt the cow would get up when she was good and ready and not before.

Ben glanced up from where he was kneeling. 'Do you want to have a look at her?' he asked, and moved over, indicating a space for Gina to kneel.

Still somewhat aggrieved by the fact that he hadn't allowed her to help earlier, Gina nodded and indulged herself in a full examination of the cow under the scrutiny of

Harvey and his men.

'No fracture of the pelvis,' she murmured as her fingers worked over the back, 'and she's moving those rear legs to get herself comfortable...'

'Which indicates the nerve supply is undamaged,' Ben added in agreement.

'And I can't feel any hip dislocation.'

'The common presenting sign in most of these conditions is when a cow won't get up, true, but I feel we can rule that out.' Ben paused. 'So the alternatives are leaving her alone or bringing in a sling and hoisting her up.'

Gina nodded. 'I'd go for calling her bluff.'

Ben smiled vaguely. 'You would, would you? That's a pretty confident attitude to take.'

'I feel pretty confident about making it,' Gina agreed, thinking what a fool she would look if things went wrong. 'If we raise her with a sling she might go down again. If she gets up under her own steam, she'll stay up.'

'*If* she gets up,' Ben grimaced.

Ignoring his scepticism, Gina went on, 'She needs to be kept comfortable, her straw changed and her milk withdrawn twice a day.' She glanced at Harvey who was standing in front of his helpers, his forehead in a deep pleat under the cloth-cap. 'What do you think, Harvey? You'll be looking after her.'

Harvey shrugged half-heartedly. 'She

could be having us on. Always was a damn lazy animal.'

There was a ripple of amusement as Gina stood up. 'You know, in here, where she can't see the rest of the herd, she might change her mind about lying around all day, become pretty bored with life.'

Ben stood up too, raising his dark eyebrows. 'All right. We'll try it your way.'

Drawing a long breath, she prayed she was on the right track. It would be a terrible blow if she wasn't; Ben would have every reason to feel justified in his suspicion of her. If her first attempt at large-animal diagnosis were to end in failure, and rather a large failure at that, it wouldn't help her prestige among the farmers either.

'Will you take a look at my other milkers, just to be sure there's no more mastitis?' Harvey asked as the group began to disperse.

'We'll be along in half a mo, Harvey,' Ben told him, gathering his equipment.

When the men had left and they were alone, Ben smiled sardonically at her. 'I hope you know what you're doing, convincing Harvey like that.'

She looked at him in amazement. 'I didn't convince him! I asked him what he thought.'

'They all heard what you said. You've got a pretty good technique, I must say.'

'That's hardly fair ... you asked me to examine her. You wanted to know what I thought. I wasn't trying to employ a "technique". Besides, if you think differently, you've only got to say.'

He watched her carefully. 'Far be it for me to object in view of such a confident diagnosis. Just answer me this; why are you so sure?'

She hesitated, for how could one explain instinct? 'I'm as sure as I can be ... because I've given her a full clinical examination and established the facts. Going on the evidence of those facts combined with what, in training, we were encouraged to develop as intuition, I formed my opinion.'

He shrugged and began to walk away, leaving her staring after him. So this was the way it was going to be between them, was it? Better, she supposed, that she knew how the land lay. And, pulling back her shoulders, she walked after him... That cow would get up, damn it. She would!

'I saw you talking with Viv,' Ben said casually as they drove home. They had checked the rest of the herd and it had been tiring work, but she resisted the temptation to ease her position in the seat.

'Yes. She seemed to know quite a lot about me,' Gina said pointedly.

'That sounds like Viv.' He laughed. 'I probably did mention you were starting with us.' He glanced at her and added,

'She's an unusual woman, isn't she?'

Gina shrugged. 'I really couldn't say. We didn't speak for very long.'

'Wasn't your intuition working at the time?' he asked mockingly and she felt her blood grow warm.

'Intuition is hardly necessary with a client,' Gina answered frostily. 'I'm quite sure if there are any relevant details you want me to know about the farm you'll tell me.'

'That sounds very businesslike. Relevant details ... let me see...'

'I didn't mean–'

'Well, to satisfy your curiosity–' he grinned, casting her a wry glance '–soon after I came here we took the Armitages on... I accepted all the large-animal work I could get until I went into partnership with Julian and we started the branch practice, shifting most of the farm work to Rowhams. But the Armitages wanted to stay here. Reggie Armitage was always a bit of a handful. The divorce was all very civilised though, and Viv came out of it pretty well, with the house and the farm. Harvey was installed as manager and Reggie, I believe, lives in the South of France now.'

'Mrs Armitage has never married again?'

'Viv's a very independent woman and a very gregarious one,' he told her swiftly. 'As long as I've known her she's enjoyed her freedom, but she has lots of friends. I wouldn't think she would give it up for any man.'

After this afternoon, Gina found herself unable to agree. She pressed herself back in the seat and concentrated on the swift rush of hedgerow. Tiredness must be a contributory factor to her state of irritation and, expelling a long, slow breath, she was more than pleased to see the lane come into view.

'You're stiff, aren't you?' he asked as they climbed out. 'I prescribe a long hot soak this evening. Heat is the best balm for backache.'

She blanched, realising he had seen and recognised the tension in her face.

'I'm getting to read the signs.' He grinned. 'And don't worry, I'm not going to give you a lecture; just do as you're told for once.'

She nodded, aware of his concern, and, feeling pink stealing into her cheeks under his scrutiny, turning away.

Strong fingers wrapped themselves around her wrist.

'There's – er – one thing more. I should have said earlier...'

She frowned at him, her heart racing, though his face was softened by the grey eyes still regarding her with concern.

'I had a phone call yesterday ... from Mrs Forbuoys.'

'Oh!' Gina was sure it was more trouble as her pulses ran hectically under the pressure of his fingers.

'It seems I was ... hasty. Mrs Forbuoys explained how she barged into your consulting room on Monday because she was so worried about Archie. She asked me to apologise on her behalf and to say that since taking your advice she's had no problem at all in giving the insulin.'

Gina took a small breath, relieved beyond words, though, now she had resigned herself to his attitude, his admission came as rather a surprise.

They stood facing one another in the growing darkness. His eyes swept over her and his fingers still lay around the curve of her wrist. She had no name for what she was feeling, too disturbed by an intense awareness of the man to give her emotions a name. A panic ran in her veins, the truth of what she felt a shifting, uncertain shape in her mind. She tried to break free of the moment, rouse herself, but he too seemed caught and his fingers lay unmoving around her wrist.

'Thank you ... f-for ... for telling me,' she stammered.

'Credit where credit is due,' he murmured and then he smiled, his face warm, his hooded eyes gazing languidly on her. 'You had better get into that bath,' he said huskily and his fingers dropped from around her wrist, freeing her.

He seemed to be so different, Gina thought

with shock. He could be two different men ... the distanced, cynical employer and the kind and caring man whom she was looking at now.

'Goodnight, Ben,' she said, moving away and as she went she was sure she could feel his eyes playing on her back, until she turned at the annexe door and saw his tall form in the dusk, striding towards the practice.

CHAPTER FOUR

Shaken, Gina took Ben's advice and bathed, trying not to dwell on their last few moments together. Tonight had shown a side of him she had not expected, and it had caught her unawares. She was unable to prevent the rise of emotion in her at his concern for her well-being, but she was afraid there was something more lying under the surface which she did not understand.

Which she didn't want to understand.

Their clash of personalities, she decided, as she lay soaking, was preferable to the peculiar light-headed sensation she had felt as he had held her wrist, his fingers seeming to throb as her skin tingled beneath his touch. And those grey eyes, the way he'd looked at her...

But no, she mustn't distort what had happened. Concern was what he had shown, plain and simple, just as he might have shown for an injured or suffering animal!

She was in pensive mood as she wrapped herself in a thick white towelling robe and dried her long dark hair. Reaching out for two small combs to hold it back in place, inadvertently she knocked them behind the set of drawers. It was not a heavy piece of furniture and she managed to shift it. Her combs lay, with several other items, on the floor.

She knelt slowly, turning them over. An old birthday card with 'Happy Birthday Grandmother' printed in delicate silver letters on the front, several shop receipts ... and a couple of snapshots.

Gina blew a fine layer of dust from the photographs. One was of a family relaxing in a garden together. A slim young woman dressed in jeans and a sun-top had Harriet's fine, blondish cropped hair and heart-shaped face. Harriet herself, aged perhaps six or seven, sat astride her father's broad shoulders. Gina steeled herself to look again as she slipped her eyes to Ben. He was laughing too, his face transformed into almost unfamiliar lines, carefree and relaxed.

The other snap was undoubtedly Sarah, just head and shoulders, the kind of photograph any mother might keep inside her purse of a dearly loved daughter. Shuffling the snaps and receipts inside the birthday card, Gina slipped them into the bottom drawer with shaky hands and for a moment couldn't move, couldn't breathe. This, she told herself in shocked amazement at her own reaction, was what you got when you opened Pandora's Box! Yes, she thought emptily, Sarah had been beautiful ... as she had imagined, a mirror image of Harriet.

The distinctly queasy feeling in her stomach forced her into the kitchen. A light meal would probably help ... but, discovering she had no appetite, she tried to satisfy the gnawing feeling behind her ribs with a milky drink.

Retiring early was a decision she regretted as she tossed and turned and finally flicked on the bedside light at a quarter to three. Her mind seemed to be fuelled with the alternating pictures of Ben and Sarah and Harriet.

Why was she being haunted by Ben's past? It was none of her business. The man meant nothing to her and yet she seemed to be drawn into his life...

Gina turned to a well-thumbed novel for distraction and propped herself up on pillows to read, but, by the time her alarm went off at seven in the morning, the book had tumbled to the floor, her neck ached from the unnatural angle at which she had drifted off and her sleep had been copious with shadowy figures.

She was on duty for Saturday morning surgery, assisted by Bev. Shaking off the unpleasant sensation the broken night had left her with, she was relieved to find a client already awaiting her in Reception. Mrs Timothy carried Su-Ling, a Pekingese, in her arms into Gina's consulting-room.

'Su-Ling is in pain,' Mrs Timothy told her. 'She's walking most peculiarly.'

Gina had studied the X-rays and, after discussing them with Stuart, was left with no option but to have to tell her client the dog needed surgery.

'I'm afraid I have to advise you to bring Su-Ling in for an operation Mrs Timothy.' She considered a detailed explanation of the complicated surgery, but dismissed the idea, unclipping the X-ray, tracing a finger over the spinal cord and saying simply, 'If you look here, you can see the space between the two vertebrae at the front part of her neck. This is narrower than the spaces lower down and there's some disc protrusion lower in her spine. In simple language, Mrs Timothy, the discs of her spine are crumbling.'

Her client looked desolate. 'I didn't expect ... well, I suppose I was too frightened to think of that possibility. Now I have to face it...'

Gina touched her arm sympathetically. 'My colleague Stuart Roberts will be doing the operation. He's our small-animal specialist and very capable. We thought ... if you decide to go ahead ... early Tuesday?'

Mrs Timothy was stricken, her mouth trembling. Gina wished she could be more optimistic, but there were no guarantees she could offer to make her client's decision any easier. Though only six years of age and not too old for the operation, Su-Ling's convalescence in itself would be tiresome for

Mrs Timothy, let alone her companion, even if the operation was entirely successful.

'I suppose there's no choice?' the elderly lady asked nervously.

Gina shook her head. 'No ... I'm afraid not. Su-Ling is in pain ... surgery is the only way to relieve it.'

Cradling Su-Ling in her arms, Mrs Timothy sighed and managed a small smile. 'I understand. Poor Su-Ling. I wish I were having the operation instead. Animals can't speak, they can't complain and here am I, frightened selfishly because I'm afraid to lose her.' She paused, trying to regain her composure, then nodded slowly. 'We'll be here on Tuesday ... and thank you. I know she'll be in safe hands.'

It was, Gina thought when alone, an awe-inspiring responsibility to be given charge of a life. How much more must doctors feel for their patients? she wondered. A thought which had occurred to her many times lately. The disadvantage here was the inability to predict to the client. The patient, though suffering, was blissfully unaware of the hand of fate ... but, in the case of humans, the intellect, in ill health, must be the greatest disadvantage.

Ben's footfall hardly disturbed her as she pondered, deep in thought, over the X-rays.

'Problems?' he asked and she nodded, handing him the X-rays, surprised to see him in the surgery on Saturday morning.

Relating the story to him, she studied his face as he looked at the details, the set of the strong square jaw, the thick-fringed dark lashes of the heavily hooded eyes. Sarah's face came back to mind too – the fair skin and pale beauty. They must have made an imposing couple...

He looked up, seeming to catch her stare, and she lowered her eyes, the annoying flush which beset her so often creeping over her cheeks.

'The possibility is if one or two discs go others are likely to follow suit,' he murmured.

'Yes ... yes, I'd thought of that and discussed it with Stuart. We were considering how much to tell Mrs Timothy. She's quite frail – very close to her pet...'

He nodded. 'What did you decide?'

'I was in two minds today. Then I thought it best not to agitate her over the weekend in case her anxiety connected to Su-Ling. So in the end I decided I'd keep it to the minimum.'

He smiled in approval. 'I'm sure you did the right thing. Normally, it's a straightforward enough op ... but...'

'Su-Ling could have complications.' She sighed.

'Stuart will only find out when he takes a look,' Ben confirmed. 'Depending on what he finds, he'll either go ahead or wait and speak to Mrs Timothy. It's an interesting case. It would be a good idea if you could assist Stuart and see for yourself.'

She nodded, distracted by yet another thought. Hesitantly she asked, 'I don't suppose there's any news from Harvey?'

He shook his head. 'None at all, I'm afraid. Still, early days yet ... which brings me to why I'm here. The kittens. There won't be anyone here after you go at twelve and Harry's at home this afternoon to amuse them.'

'I'll give you a hand,' Gina said and, trying to forget about Harvey, walked with him to the recovery-room, gently awakening the three tabby kittens from sleep, transferring them into a cat-box.

'How's the back this morning?' Ben asked as he collected a litter tray and some granular litter, frowning at her with deeply set grey eyes.

She smiled. 'Much better. I took your advice. Soaked until I felt like a wrinkled prune.' She saw him laughing as he picked up the cat-box, grateful that he did not show an obvious gleam of satisfaction at the disappointment written on her face when he told her there was no news from Harvey. Suddenly realising she was staring after the tall figure striding down the corridor, her thoughts were helpfully distracted by a man passing Ben, urging a reluctant-looking

Dobermann towards her consulting-room.

'I'm just wondering if there's something physically wrong with him,' Mr Billingham explained, tugging his dog over the threshold. 'He whines all the time.'

Chessel, it evolved, was eating well and taking exercise. Gina checked his glands, ears and eyes, sounded his heart and looked carefully through the short, glossy coat, which was in perfect condition.

When the examination was over and she began to reassure his owner, Chessel began a low grumble in his throat which rose to a discontented whine.

'You see? As soon as he's not the centre of attention he starts. It drives the wife and me to distraction.'

Gina nodded sympathetically. 'I think Chessel has a behavioural problem. The best course of action will be to take him to a dog-handler, a specialist in his breed who will be able to help you. At least I can reassure you he's perfectly well, in fact in the peak of condition. I'll have our nurse give you the telephone number of someone who can help.'

Mr Billingham led the morose Chessel to the door. 'Well, that's put my mind at rest ... but goodness knows why he does it.'

Gina grinned. 'The mystery lies in the breeding, I believe. I'm afraid Dobermann are known to be indomitable grizzlers. When we have them in recovery after an operation we almost have to wear earplugs!'

Mr Billingham sighed, shaking his head. 'And he's only three ... does it get worse?'

'Not necessarily; he's young enough to be retrained. The story goes that the man who started the breed was a tax-collector, a Herr Dobermann. He decided his Rottweiler dogs weren't frightening his poor clients enough as on the whole, when unprovoked, they are rather quiet, so he decided to cross them with an unknown hound ... the villain of the piece!'

Mr Billingham smiled wryly and led Chessel away, still grizzling, as a young man and his small daughter, who was carrying a puppy, entered her consulting-room. Gina carefully took the puppy and gave him an examination, finding a rupture of the belly-button; but it was slight. Reassuring them that the condition was temporary and, in due course, the opening in the abdominal wall would close, she suggested another visit in several weeks' time.

The morning eventually over with, Gina went back to the flat and, as Stuart was on call, decided to make the most of the after-noon. Browsing round the shops in Poole, she bought flowers for her mother and stocked up with grocery provisions. Unable to resist phoning from the car phone, her mind inevitably drawn back to Harvey, she received the news from Vicki that Harvey had not rung in.

The following morning she decided she would go and see Harvey herself. Though Sunday was her day off and she intended to visit her parents, she couldn't relax until she had, at least, examined the cow again.

She was just about to leave when the phone rang. 'We've had some good news, Gina,' Vicki told her. 'Harvey's rung to say the cow is up this morning and eating. All she needs is someone to take a look at her udder to make sure it's healing.'

'I'll go immediately,' Gina said with relief. 'Don't trouble Stuart, because I'm going past the Armitages *en route* to my parents.'

'Are you sure? I mean, Stuart is officially on call this weekend.'

'Perfectly. Just put my name alongside the visit.'

Gina drove in a happy frame of mind to Armitage Farm. Harvey was waiting for her and together they checked the cow who looked none the worse for wear. Her udder had healed well and her milk was without taint. Talking with Harvey, Gina realised just how much she enjoyed the flavour of farm work again. Companion animals were engrossing and ever presenting new problems, but there was something invigorating about dealing with large animals and with the farmers themselves.

Because she spent more time than she

should with Harvey, it was after lunch when she reached her parents and ate a delayed Sunday roast. Ebulliently she relayed her triumph of the cow as they dined, amusing her parents with the descriptions of her first cases at work.

It was evening when she headed back through the Purbecks. She was feeling on a high, and the thought occurred to her that Ben must now know from Harvey what had happened. Should she call briefly at the cottage?

The thought of seeing his face ... but no, she decided as she drove; it would be purely self-satisfaction. Monday would come soon enough. But as she neared home, with the evening stretching before her, she slowly gave in to the temptation. She could ask Harriet how the kittens were, too...

Why not?

And so she found herself pushing open the wicket gate towards the cottage after parking the Fiesta.

She pulled back her small shoulders, her dark hair tucked neatly into a heather-coloured ribbon at the nape of her neck, her cheeks flushed from the stimulation of her day. Lights were blazing from the cottage, the upstairs ones, too, in Harriet's bedroom.

She raised the heavy lion's head on the cottage door but, before she allowed it to drop, shadows cast out from the front-room window caused her to hesitate. Two figures silhouetted against the light were displayed as Gina laid the brass head gently down against the wood, making no sound.

Horror swept over her. What a fool she was making of herself! She quickly turned on her heel and hurried up the garden path, closing the wicket gate quietly behind her.

The next morning, Vivienne Armitage discreetly left the cottage at six-thirty.

Gina saw, because she was perched on the window-seat of the bay-window, gazing out on to the dusky fields. In the illumination of the outer light she watched Ben's lover hurry to her car, a dark blue saloon parked just beyond the Discovery, neither of which, in her eager anticipation last night, she had noticed.

Much later, when Gina arrived at the surgery, firmly instructing herself to concentrate on the day ahead and not the mental picture of Vivienne Armitage hurrying from the cottage, she found the front door open and Ben standing in reception. For a second her heart leapt, then, quickly, she recovered her composure.

'I'm glad you're early,' he said, disregarding the usual greetings. 'Could I have a word, Gina?' He motioned to his room and, uncertainly, slipping off her coat and hanging it up, she followed him, instantly aware of the tense atmosphere.

'Is there something wrong?' she asked, suddenly concerned.

He gestured her to sit and, as she did so, he moved across the room restlessly. With his back to her as he gazed out of the window, he seemed to be deciding on what to say.

Eventually he came to sit too. 'I wanted to talk to you before the other staff arrived.'

He could have come to talk to her in private in the annexe if it was so important ... but no, he couldn't, could he? He had been busy entertaining.

'Would you like some coffee?'

'No ... no, thanks.' She was mystified as to why her own tone of voice seemed so remote. Why was she feeling like this? Did it matter to her if his girlfriend stayed overnight and slipped out in the early hours of the morning? It was surely his affair and his alone!

'Firstly,' Ben was saying, 'Stuart rang in this morning to say he's woken with a temperature and aching limbs. He thinks he's caught Julian's bug. If he isn't back tomorrow then I will have to do any small ops booked in, but today it will just be you and me.'

She nodded.

'And the next thing; you went out to Harvey's yesterday, didn't you?'

'Yes ... the cow is on her feet. I–'

'You had no reason to visit Harvey,' he said coolly. 'Stuart was on call. He should have gone. You know that's the way it works.'

'But Harvey rang to–'

'Harvey might have rung, but it didn't mean you had to go chasing out there.'

She didn't understand him at all! 'I was concerned about the cow,' she protested. 'After all, it was I who suggested she be left recumbent. The udder had to be checked and I was going past there on my way to my parents'.'

He frowned at her. 'You're missing the point entirely, Gina! This practice doesn't hold together on each of us working as individuals – doing what we like, when we like! There are rules – and we stick to them. We work as a unit, and the sooner you get used to the idea the better!'

She sat in silence, her barely concealed anger simmering under the surface. She was just trying to do her best. But for some reason he was misinterpreting her actions.

'Do you treat all your staff like this when they try to show enthusiasm?' she asked him with contempt in her voice. 'Or are you really so upset that Gerald Gorley let you down? Am I such an inadequate understudy?'

He looked at her for a moment in silence, then said slowly, 'Is that what you think? I thought there was something. As it happens, I find you neither inadequate, nor do I class you as an understudy. But you are, in my opinion, impulsive. I told you once; this is my practice, Gina. I lay down the rules and I expect my staff to keep to them.'

The home truth caught her off guard. Was she being impulsive – too headstrong? She said hesitantly, 'Well … maybe I shouldn't have gone out to Harvey's … but, as for putting everything I have into my work, that's not such a bad thing, surely?'

'I didn't say it was.'

'Then what are you trying to say?' she asked with a spurt of irritation.

He shrugged, calmly regarding her. 'A number of things. If it were a partnership I was offering it might be different; I could understand. But you're simply the locum. You've also been distanced from practising for a long while and you won't make up that lost experience by burning yourself out.'

The blood drained from her face as she gasped, 'A partnership? What makes you think I want a partnership?'

'Don't take me the wrong way,' he added quickly. 'You did ask me to make myself plain. Now that I have, I can see I would have been wiser to keep my mouth shut.'

Trying to dismiss the involuntary lurch of her stomach muscles, she forbade herself to give in to the surge of anger threatening to overwhelm her. It was probably what he wanted – the satisfaction of being able to say she had no control either.

She took a deep breath, rose slowly and

walked to the door. 'If there's nothing more?' she asked, her violet eyes as dark as coals.

He shook his head and she swept out of the room, her cheeks going from ashen to flaring pink as fresh emotion drove into her face.

'Morning!' Vicki called cheerfully.

Gina nodded, barely seeing her through a mist of anger. In her room, with her heart thudding, she leaned for a moment on her desk, waiting for the traumatic eruption inside her to subside. A partnership? So, that was what he thought she was after. Now she understood. Her motives appeared ruthless. She sensed she represented all that he did not like in a woman, mistaking her enthusiasm for single-minded ambition!

Doing a simple job of work under Ben Cassell's roof wasn't easy. And as she managed to proceed with her day, avoiding the consulting-room next door to hers like the plague, finding relief in the afternoon when he was called out on an emergency visit, Gina arrived at the conclusion, by the time she walked home, that neither her job nor Ben Cassell's opinion of her was worth this kind of anguish and the sooner she accepted the fact the better!

Mrs Timothy arrived the next day with Su-Ling. Sleep had soothed Gina's anger and she determined, as her heart went out to the elderly lady who clung to her pet until the last moment, that today there was no way in which Ben would spark off her temper.

'She hasn't had any food or drink since yesterday, has she?' Gina asked, transferring the Pekingese to her arms.

Mrs Timothy shook her head. 'Nor have I. I've been so worried.'

Gina wished there were something of comfort she could say, but in view of the dog's condition, discretion was needed. 'Would you like to sit and rest for a while?' she asked. 'We have a small, quiet room. I could bring you a cup of tea.'

Her client looked up shakily. 'You're very kind, my dear. I do appreciate your thoughtfulness, but I'd better leave Su-Ling now. If I don't go, you'll probably find me sitting here when you go to close up.'

Su-Ling's beautiful round eyes followed her mistress's figure as she walked away. Vicki took the little dog in her arms and Gina wondered if and when Stuart would arrive.

Her question was answered almost immediately as Ben came in frowning. 'No Stuart, I'm afraid.' He sighed, looking at the Pekingese in Vicki's arms. 'We'll get morning surgery over and done with, then concentrate on Su-Ling's operation – that is, if you've nothing booked, Gina?'

'No, nothing at all.' She watched him talking to Vicki, his hand stretched out to stroke the top of Su-Ling's head, the long fingers moving compassionately over her. He was such a large man, but his touch was always gentle, caring. His manner showed no hint of yesterday's disagreement and, as he drew Gina into the conversation on the proposed operation, she was almost inclined to think their heated words had never happened. What, after all, did their quarrel amount to? Nothing that was said should interfere with their professional rapport, unless, of course, they allowed it to. And today of all days, with theatre work in front of them, it was crucial that she put all that happened behind her.

Later in the morning, as she stood beside Ben after giving Su-Ling the anaesthetic, she realised just how little she needed to worry when it came to professionalism. Ben's voice guided her expertly into the operation, his tone patient, his eyes warm ... she almost felt as though she was an extension of his fingers as he worked.

'The disc, as you know, is like a Polo mint–' he demonstrated, carefully incising '–with a soft inner core. What happens is, the centre slides up through the wall and squashes the spinal cord. Hence the traumatic pain ... the wobbly behind, as Mrs Timothy called it.'

Gina watched carefully as he revealed the area under his skilful fingers. 'Can we attempt to help her today?'

He nodded, arching the dark brows. 'I don't think there's a choice. I'm going to make a hole in the bottom of this disc and remove the soft centre.'

After successfully doing this, he glanced at Gina. 'You know, I'm going to do the whole lot in one go. It's extra surgical time ... but there's no point in having all this repeated again in another six months, maybe less.'

Gina sighed. She had expected as much. Su-Ling's spine was in a pitiful state. 'And her chances?' She ventured to ask.

'There's very little haemorrhage ... if we hit no special problems ... probably better than an eighty per cent complete recovery-rate.'

With her confidence growing she watched in admiration as his fingers dealt with the fragile fabric of Su-Ling's backbone, moving carefully along to each segment of the spine.

'How's the blood?' he asked as she dabbed at his forehead with a cloth, the concentration on his work bringing out small beads of sweat.

'Well-oxygenated and red.'

'Not long now.' His grey eyes smilingly met hers. 'Would you care to finish off?'

Aware that he was preparing an injection of heart stimulant, she began the suturing, tying and cutting off the last knot carefully. She felt no embarrassment under his professional gaze, her fingers taking the skin together carefully, the line of neat sutures barely revealing the invasive surgery below.

'Well done.' He smiled at her. 'Good to get back in the swing of things, I should imagine?'

'Yes ... very good.' She straightened up, smiling, grateful for the opportunity of working with him that had come unexpectedly her way.

'She'll need some intense post-op nursing. The surgery was a little more radical than I expected. As soon as she recovers I want to know. Are you going to keep an eye on her, or Vicki?' he asked.

'No ... I'll be here.'

He nodded, stripping off his surgical gloves. 'Let's get her into Recovery, shall we?'

Su-Ling was carefully installed in her recovery cage, a drip fitted and the heat adjusted so that the temperature of the room would be adequate for the delicate recovery.

Ben finally checked her, then smiled at Gina. 'I'm going over to the cottage if you want me – feeding the kittens for Harry.' He grinned wryly. 'She's left me with explicit instructions on what to dish up.'

Gina laughed lightly. 'She managed them over the weekend?'

'Expertly.' He frowned at her, grey eyes reflective. 'I think she was rather disappointed you didn't come in to see them.

She had some sort of idea you would.'

And bump into Vivienne Armitage? Gina thought with sudden annoyance. No, that particular lady held no allure for her!

'Why don't you come over this evening?' he suggested.

Her brows drew together as she tried to think of an excuse to refuse. 'I ... I'm not quite sure what I'm–'

'Just for an hour. Have a chat to Harry about their welfare. I've outlined what should be done, vaccinations and so forth, but I'm sure she'd much rather hear it from you.'

She had no option, it seemed. If she refused she might hurt Harriet's feelings and that was the last thing she wanted to do. Gina nodded uncertainly. 'All right. I'll come over after supper, but just for an hour.'

As she watched him arrange Su-Ling's drip, his long, agile fingers working with the tubing, Gina reflected that the Cassell household was the last place she wanted to be this evening. The morning had passed without altercation, but it seemed foolishly optimistic that an evening – if only an hour – spent in the company of her employer would ease the tension on which her nerves seemed to be sprung whenever she was with him lately.

CHAPTER FIVE

Gina curled her fingers under the warm, well-fed tummy, lifting the kitten back into her new bed. 'They will need protein, fat, vitamins and minerals, all in the right proportions. There are some good proprietary brands on the market at the moment–'

Harriet grinned, opening a cupboard to reveal a shelf full of canned and potted cat foods.

'Oh … I'm a bit late, aren't I?' Gina laughed.

'Spoilt for choice,' Ben said ruefully, his tall figure dominating the kitchen. It was strange to see him in this setting as he stacked the coffee-tray neatly. She had found herself noticing more about him on a professional level as they worked, but here in the kitchen she found an unusual absorption in following his domesticated movements. She dragged her attention back to Harriet and the three kittens, and Tabitha promptly jumped in between them, settling on Gina's lap.

'Their surrogate mum, I see,' Gina observed. 'She's very good-natured!' Gina stroked the cat as she lazily stretched out her neck. 'Don't forget to give the little one some sterilised bonemeal for calcium and yeast extract for thiamine.'

'And a teaspoonful of cod liver oil once a week,' put in Ben with a grin as he carried the coffee-tray into the hall. 'Just be sure not to over-supplement!'

Gina looked after him with amusement. 'Your father's quite right, of course. Incidentally, have you given them names?'

'Mrs Swain has: Fluff, Scamp and Tiny!'

Gina tickled Tiny under her miniature chin. 'It's very important to have them vaccinated soon. Kittens and cats can pick up three pretty serious diseases. Infectious enteritis, viral rhinotracheitis and calici virus ... or cat flu.'

Harriet wrinkled her nose. 'Poor things. Fancy coming into the world and catching flu straight away!'

'Like human babies, they need a little help from medical science to begin with. That's what's so wonderful about being in a position to offer it,' Gina said reflectively.

Harriet nodded, her eyes deepening to sea-blue, her heart-shaped face pale and wary. 'I thought you may have come over during the weekend.'

Gina felt the slow rise of colour in her cheeks. The last thing she wanted to do was admit that she had!

But too late Harriet caught her reaction.

'You did call!' she guessed astutely. 'I was up in my bedroom and I thought I heard the wicket gate go. Sunday evening, wasn't it?'

There was no way Gina could disguise her crimson flush. 'I realised you had visitors already,' she confessed uncomfortably.

'Just one,' Harriet muttered with sharp indignation. 'Vivienne Armitage. But she only wanted to see Daddy. Vivienne can't stand it when I'm around her. I cramp her style.'

'Oh, Harriet, I'm sure she really does—'

'Dislike me!' Harriet provided bitterly. 'It's true! I happened to overhear Bev and Vicki talking one day when I had to go into the surgery to see Daddy. Now that she hasn't got a husband of her own, they said, she's after marrying again and Daddy certainly fits the bill. It's just that I don't. And that's why she can't stand the sight of me!'

Gina felt her heart constrict as she thought of poor Harriet learning those painful home truths. Truths which were so undoubtedly correct, it would have been patronising even to attempt an alternative explanation. Meeting Vivienne Armitage the other day for herself, Gina had realised that the divorcee would let no other threaten the territory she had mapped out for the handsome vet and herself – and that included any female, no matter who!

Gina smothered the enormous urge to put

her arms around Harriet. But Harriet was in no mood for platitudes or hugs and it was with great relief that Gina heard Ben call them from the front room.

Later, the girl sat by the fire cross-legged and Gina sipped her coffee on the sofa. Ben lounged on the chesterfield, watching them both as they talked about the changes at St Mary's. Occasionally she caught his stare, the grey eyes silently probing her face.

'Did Daddy tell you Nana is coming to stay soon?' Harriet asked suddenly. 'You'll like Nana,' she went on, regardless of her father's frown. 'When we moved here after Mummy died, she came with us. I was only nine at the time, you see.'

Gina glanced at Ben; his deeply concerned eyes were fixed on his daughter. Harriet showed no sign of distress when talking of her mother, but Gina guessed at the subconscious reaction, Harriet's face flushed and her eyes moving hesitantly across to her father. 'Nana used to look after me a lot when I was young because Mummy always had so much to do, with the practice getting busier and busier.'

The telephone rang and Harriet jumped up. 'I'll get it! It might be Jenny ... a friend of mine ... she said she'd ring tonight about some maths homework.'

When Harriet had gone, Ben put his cup down and smiled apologetically at Gina.

'I'm sorry you're being treated to Harriet's potted version of the family history. It's not usual she's so chatty. As I told you, she's very selective about people.' He shrugged, his face concerned. 'What Harry was saying about her mother... I have to qualify her remarks by explaining that Sarah and I were both trying to get the practice well-established in the early years. It's true I thought Sarah might be able to take things easier when Harriet came along ... perhaps work part-time ... but she was a very dedicated vet. She built up a firm rapport with her clients and patients and took her role in the business very seriously. It was difficult for her ... and, as Audrey was always willing to fill in...'

'Jenny said Maureen hasn't a clue either!' Harriet announced as she burst back into the room. 'That makes three of us at least who didn't finish off our maths revision for tomorrow's tests.'

'I hope you're not serious!' Ben frowned.

'I'm only teasing!' Harriet sighed petulantly.

But somewhere in that light-hearted tease there was a profound clue, Gina reflected, to a very confused adolescent. Silent cries for attention ... oh, yes, she remembered them so well herself. But in Harriet's case she had only one parent left to her. And if Sarah had been as busy as Ben had suggested, perhaps family had taken second place, so adding to Harriet's resentment after her death. Added to which, there was now the ever-present threat of Vivienne. The result was a very threatened Harriet who wouldn't admit to her father what was wrong, appearing instead to be a typical sulky and temperamental teenager with a strong dislike of animals.

By the evidence of the snaps Gina had found in the flat it was hard to believe there had been trouble in Eden. But then, how many photographs did her own parents have in overflowing albums which depicted happy scenes behind which there was disruption – caused in the main by her rebellion in adolescence and her father's frustrated attempts at dealing with it?

Ben was standing over her. 'Gina? More coffee?'

'Oh ... no ... thank you. I really must go now.'

'I'll walk back with you, Gina,' Harriet suggested easily.

Gina glanced questioningly at Ben.

'Don't stay out gossiping,' he conceded with a grin. 'You've those tests in the morning, remember, Harry.'

Ben's daughter talked rapidly as she walked with Gina along the garden path. The sky was bright with stars and a full moon lit up the shadows with a soft grey light. The subjects covered were so wide-ranging that Gina smiled, remembering just how it was to be fifteen, on the very brink of life. Harriet reminded her so much of herself, vulnerable yet trying to be assertive with her father, trying to prove her independence and all the time needing that supportive parental love which was so precious.

'I've had a lovely evening, Harriet. The kittens are lucky to be alive and so well, thanks to your care.' She eventually found her key in her pocket, inserted it in the lock, and the door swung open.

For a moment a slow groaning rolled around the little porch, then there was an enormous bang which made the door shudder under her grasp.

'What in heaven's name was that?' Gina whispered, peering into the flat and switching on the inner light; she thought immediately of burglars.

'Oh, goodness!' Harriet frowned. 'It sounds like the plumbing. I think you've got an air lock. Nana used to have them when she was here. Daddy has to do something to the pipes.'

Gina listened to the medley of noises running throughout the annexe. 'At lease it's not intruders.' She laughed, quite relieved. 'I'm sure it can wait until the morning.'

Another resounding bang cut her short and Harriet shook her head. 'I'm afraid it can't. I'll run and get him. Goodnight, Gina!'

Gina watched her go, in two minds as to whether to suggest she just switch off the central heating completely. It would save Ben having to come at this time of night, but Harriet had disappeared and so she went in, listening to the extraordinary whistling and groaning. She had no idea what to do about air locks, a faint memory of the central heating at her parents' place conjuring only the vision of her father's legs disappearing up into the attic and a few expletives to follow.

'Mind if I take a look?' Ben stood in the porch looking in.

Gina smiled. 'Of course ... go ahead. Harriet said it was an air lock. Does it happen often?'

'Only at the most inconvenient of times.' He grinned as he walked past her. 'I thought we had it all sorted out. Before you moved in a firm came to service the boiler and check the piping. I'll go through to the box-room...'

The room was very small with an airing cupboard in one corner. Ben opened the door and got down on his knees, frowning at the tank and the curious arrangement of pipes leading from it. 'Blessed thing had some new-fangled plastic bits put in,' she heard him mutter.

She knew from experience that it was best

to be out of earshot when men attempted repairs and she began her escape to the front room, when Ben called out, 'You haven't seen a spanner around at all? The plumber said he left one which fitted, said he left it on the shelving…'

Gina remembered that she had indeed found a spanner and after making a mental note to return it to Ben along with the photographs, she had, of course, forgotten completely. 'Yes … I didn't realise it was for the tank. I put it up here … top shelf.' She pulled a chair over and tried to squeeze it in between Ben's large body and the open door. Though the angle was precarious she managed to get one foot on the seat.

'Be careful, Gina!'

But Ben's warning came too late. She began wobbling and clutched at the slatted shelving, causing them to slide together in a rush.

Ben sprang to his feet, catching her before she hit the ground. The shelving clattered on top of them and she felt his large hand press her head into his chest, protecting her from the blunt ends of the wood.

With her heart pumping erratically, she waited for the noise to subside, which it didn't, because it was her own pulse beating like a drum in her ears.

'That was a silly thing to do!' he said huskily, his arms tight around her, his large hand still cupping her head.

'I ... I was trying to reach...' Her words faded out as she looked up at him.

For seconds they stared at one another. Was this actually happening to her? Was she really in his arms? Then slowly his mouth came down. His lips were soft yet enquiring and her mouth opened in hesitant response as her eyes fluttered closed, his hands bringing her body closer to him. Her arms went around his neck. The thought rushed through her bemused mind that she had wanted this to happen from the very first moment she had seen this man, wanted to discover what it was like to be kissed by him.

Now it was happening.

Her fingertips found the hard, muscled neck and the tangle of thick coppery hair. She felt pierced with an unfamiliar excitement as his kiss grew deeper, their bodies hot as the intensity grew between them. His fingers roamed her hair, her chintzy scarf, which she had tied around her head, falling to the floor.

She moaned softly, not sure any more whether the orchestration of sound in her ears was from the house or her own hammering heart as his hand slid under the heavy weight of her dark hair and trailed down to the sensitive small of her back. She could feel the heat in his fingers through her silk blouse, her senses alight to his touch.

No man had evoked the response which her body seemed to be making under his touch; nothing had ever been like this before, and her mouth opened again under the pressure of his lips.

He murmured her name and her eyes flashed open as though she was waking from a deep dream-state. Almost before she could take a breath he looked at her, confusion and hunger written in the deep grey eyes, so startlingly that for a moment they were locked by their own intensity of thought.

She couldn't think ... couldn't move; her body trembled. Then she stiffened as they heard a movement outside, followed by Harriet's call.

He let go of her, the hooded eyes flicking open wide. Running his hand through the tousled hair which had fallen across his forehead, he called, 'Harry? We're in here.'

Gina stepped back, her legs like air. He bent down and lifted the chair, collecting the slats of wood and stacking them to one side.

'My goodness ... what's been happening?' Harriet frowned as she came in.

'Oh ... the shelves collapsed,' Gina said, feeling the colour sweep up to her cheeks. 'It was my fault; I tried to balance on the chair to reach the top shelf.'

'Do you need any help?' Harriet asked.

'No ... I can do it now. The spanner fell

down with the shelving,' Ben said, leaning back on his haunches. A slow hiss came from the pipe as he turned the spanner. When water began to trickle out he jerked the tool backwards.

'That's better,' Harriet said cheerfully. 'The noise has stopped.'

Gina was afraid to meet Ben's eyes as he looked up. 'I'm sorry ... I seem to have caused havoc,' she apologised.

'Nana had exactly the same problem,' Harriet dismissed. 'Daddy said he was going to have new plumbing throughout the annexe but he never got around–'

'You shouldn't have any more trouble,' Ben interrupted, propelling Harriet out of the room towards the front door.

'Goodnight, Gina.'

It was almost as though what happened – hadn't happened. He behaved so normally! Gina wondered if it had all been some terrible figment of her imagination as he jerked the latch open.

But at the door, as Harriet was halfway down the garden path, he turned back and said softly, 'I'm sorry, Gina... I'll speak to you in the morning.'

Then he was gone.

She closed the door and rested against it, shutting her eyes. How could he have pulled himself together so quickly? As for her, she could hardly speak ... hardly think! His face had been so utterly normal when he'd looked at her, no one would have guessed at the intensity of that embrace. Even now she hardly believed it herself.

Shame made her cheeks burn with colour as she thought about the way she had responded. No man had ever – not even Kieron whom she thought she had loved – made her feel so... She couldn't find the words...

'Stop it, Gina!' she told herself angrily.

It was just an impulse, something that happened because sometimes those sort of things did happen. Physical chemistry was an unreliable force and it had caught them both unguarded. Ben Cassell was not her type of man. She must be crazy even to give the incident a second thought.

Gradually she began to think more calmly. After her accident and her final splitting up with Kieron she had concentrated on getting well and back to work, hadn't she? So it was to some extent understandable that her emotions had run away with her tonight, a spontaneous response which was unfortunate but surely not the end of the world?

His attraction ... and there was no denying that physically he was a very attractive man ... was only surface-deep. They had both been caught by the sexual impulse that had sparked like electricity between them. She would have to guard against it ever happening again, now that she was aware of what could happen. But there was no sense in being over-concerned. For men, a casual involvement meant nothing. He certainly wasn't attracted to her in any real sense, the way he was, for instance, to Vivienne Armitage.

At the thought of Vivienne, Gina felt disturbed, even uncomfortable, and relegated her introspection to the back of her mind. She took a shower and made herself study some notes she had made during the day.

Whatever Ben had to say tomorrow, she would be well-prepared now that she had thought it all out sensibly.

The next morning a nurse called Lyn Browning was on duty. Vicki and Bev had time off and, although Lyn did not live at the nurses' quarters but in Poole with her husband and young son, she had worked part-time for Ben for several years.

Gina was settling into her room, wondering when Ben would make an appearance, when the first client was ushered in by Lyn. The nurse drew her eyebrows together in concern as she looked around Gina's door. 'Gina, we've a really unusual first patient – a ferret. Mr Howe thinks it's sick and I'm inclined to agree, so I've put them down in the isolation-room for safety's sake.'

Gina nodded. 'Fine, Lyn. I'll come straight away. Is Ben in yet?'

'No ... should I ring through to the cottage?'

Gina shook her head quickly. The last person she was looking forward to meeting this morning was Ben. Last night seemed like a dream, something that could not possibly have taken place and yet... Gina blinked hard and smiled uncertainly. 'No, don't bother him. I'm sure we'll manage.'

'As a matter of fact, my uncle used to keep ferrets,' Lyn told Gina as they hurried down to the isolation-room. 'He began to have his ferrets vaccinated after a virus killed off some of his females – jills, aren't they called? I just happened to see one of them when they were ill and I have a horrible feeling this one looks very much like it.'

Gina nodded, following Lyn into the small room at the end of the corridor.

After introductions were made, Mr Howe gingerly opened the box and they were met by a terrible smell.

'My son found it yesterday. Strangely enough the poor thing didn't look too bad, but today it has developed these swollen feet and runny eyes and this morning, when I looked, it had been sick.'

'You found it yesterday?'

'Yes. Darren discovered it on his way home from school, trapped in an old barrel. The boys got it into a sack. It was pretty exhausted, didn't make too much of an

113

attempt to struggle. Darren wouldn't have known but some dogs were barking, trying to get into the barrel. He brought it home and showed it to his mum. She wouldn't have it near the house, so he put it in the garden shed. I managed to get it in the box and brought it straight here. Doesn't look right to me.'

Gina opened the lid and, to her dismay, recognised immediately what was wrong. She had seen the disease in dogs and all the signs were presented here: the badly infected face and feet, and evidence of diarrhoea and sickness.

'Here's Ben,' Lyn said behind her. 'I'll go and get him.'

'Thanks, Lyn, but I think it's probably distemper and there will be little either of us can do.'

'Distemper?' queried Mr Howe, frowning. 'I thought only dogs got that.'

'No, I'm afraid not. Distemper affects ferrets too,' Gina sighed.

'The lad's going to be heartbroken when I tell him. He had some idea about nursing it back to health. We think someone's breeding them just for money .. the word gets around with the kids, you know.'

Gina nodded. 'I'm afraid there are un-scrupulous people who breed and sell animals without compunction, not only ferrets but dogs and reptiles too. Things like exotic animals and birds have a value, you see, and there are some who just want to make quick cash. Incidentally, have you any other animals at home, Mr Howe?'

He shook his head. 'Our old dog died a couple of months back; that's why Darren was so keen to keep this. Why ... is it catching, this disease?'

'I'm afraid it is ... oh, good morning, Ben.'

'Good morning.' He nodded briefly at her and acknowledged Mr Howe.

'Mr Howe's son found a trapped ferret yesterday. I think it's probably distemper.' She had been preparing herself for their first meeting after last night, but all conscious planning went out of her mind as she saw Ben's face change. The animal's distraught condition had the same effect on him, she knew. His face darkened and his grey eyes met hers.

'I'm afraid there's no doubt,' he said and she nodded, glancing at Mr Howe.

'What can you do for it ... there must be something?' the man asked as he looked at them both.

Ben shook his head. 'This animal is very sick indeed. It will be kinder to put the poor creature out of its misery.'

Mr Howe stood back, giving in to a long sigh. 'I was too late.'

Ben said kindly, 'No, not in one sense. Distemper is highly infectious and there is a vaccine, but I couldn't have administered it. Vaccines are given to prevent disease, not cure. You will have saved him hours of agony, if it's any consolation.' He leaned across and took the box. 'And, I must impress on you, anyone who has handled the ferret must ensure that their hands are thoroughly disinfected and wherever he has been must be kept thoroughly cleaned out.'

'Oh, the wife made Darren wash his hands, all right. And me too. But if you've got somewhere I could wash them now.'

Gina led him out of the room and in the opposite direction to Ben who disappeared to alleviate the creature's suffering quietly.

Gina saw Mr Howe before he left, reminding him, 'Don't forget your garden shed. Make sure you disinfect it and perhaps impress on Darren that if he should hear anything about ferret breeding or bartering, then it would be wise to get in touch with the RSPCA. One of their investigators will almost certainly go along to inspect.'

Mr Howe nodded. 'And what about payment? The ferret wasn't mine, but I'm willing to pay you–'

'That's quite all right,' Ben interrupted as he came back into Reception. 'It was lucky your son found him. Thank you for taking the trouble to bring him in.'

'It was a male, was it?' the man asked.

'Yes ... they're called hobs. In actual fact

males aren't so popular because they don't produce young. Ferreters often borrow a hob from a friend for mating their jills. This one may have escaped as it was being transported for that purpose.'

'I think I'll stick to dogs and get the lad a puppy after today,' Mr Howe said, rather white-faced.

'In which case,' Ben added with an encouraging smile, 'bring the puppy in for his vaccinations promptly, won't you?'

As the door closed behind him, Ben turned to Gina. 'I think I'll put in my own report to the RSPCA. Whenever will people learn that keeping any animal carries with it a responsibility, a very big one? And those who breed just for the sake of making a few pitiful pounds, ignoring the dangers of a disease like distemper...' He stopped, exasperated, his lips twisted with anger.

She sighed, touching his arm gently because she felt exactly the same way. For a moment she forgot about everything, until his eyes met hers and she jerked her hand away, realising what she had done.

'I'd – er – better see to my next patient,' she said, only for him to block her way.

'Gina ... I must speak to–'

'Gina!' Lyn called from her consulting-room.

Gina saw his expression change and, finding no appropriate words to say, she paused

117

no more than a few seconds, finally hurrying off to answer Lyn's call.

In her room she found a woeful-looking basset with a wound on his rump, the recipient of another, larger dog's aggression. Byron's brown eyes were red at the lower lids, making his face even sadder than normal, and Gina bent down to examine the wound on his side as he gazed up at her; she stroked him gently, careful to avoid the wound.

'We'll have to put three or four stitches in this, I'm afraid,' she told his owner.

The lady, unable to disguise her squeamishness, left Gina and Lyn to lift Byron on to the treatment table while she retired to the waiting-room.

'Some people!' Lyn sighed. 'I could never leave my pet if he needed medical attention!'

Gina secretly agreed, but said generously, 'On the other hand, it's better the lady knows her limitations ... you know what it's like if an owner faints!'

'Don't I just. Oh ... come on, Byron; relax, my sweet; you're not going to feel a thing,' Lyn coaxed as she cleaned the wound thoroughly.

'What's the damage?' Ben said in a deep voice as he suddenly walked in.

'Fine ... so far,' Gina murmured, surprised at his appearance. 'A few stitches needed, that's all.'

'There are a couple of clients in Reception, Lyn,' he said as he bent over Byron. 'They've brought their dogs in before and I – er – need their case histories. Perhaps I'll give Gina a hand while you sort out the paperwork for me?'

'Oh … right!' Lyn hesitantly relinquished care of Byron to Ben and peeled off her gloves. 'I'll be as quick as I can.'

'No hurry,' Ben answered as she left. 'Doesn't look too bad,' he said, frowning, and Gina paused.

'No, it doesn't, does it?' she agreed tensely. 'No muscle damage, so it's just a straight-forward local anaesthetic.'

Gina put the anaesthetic into the wound and Byron blinked his large, doleful eyes.

'Gina … about last night,' Ben said huskily as they waited for it to take effect. She looked up at him, knowing in her mind how she had planned to respond to this moment, but her mind was a blank.

'It's forgotten,' she demurred, seizing on the first thing that came into her head. 'Forgotten entirely.'

He stiffened beside her, unwilling to let the matter drop. 'I'm concerned … about the way I left last night. I couldn't stay and talk to you because–'

'Of Harriet,' Gina provided sharply. 'Yes, of course.'

'Yes, because of Harriet … but also

because I wanted time to talk to you ... alone...'

'I understand you didn't want to embarrass Harriet,' she said, her violet eyes cool.

'Nor compromise you.'

'Ben ... let's not resort to making excuses. It was a spur-of-the-moment ... mistake ... for want of a better word. Shall we drop the subject?'

'You don't understand,' he ground out with emphasis. 'Give me a chance to–'

'Look out!' Gina warned as Byron tried to leap. Ben caught him just as he began his descent, hoisting him back on to the table with a quiet curse between his teeth, his face red.

'Your patient is in your room and the notes are on your desk,' Lyn said as she walked back in, then, frowning at Ben's dishevelment, she asked curiously, 'Goodness, are you all right?'

Ben nodded brusquely. 'He's heavier than I thought. Keep hold of him; he's pretty athletic for a basset.' He stood aside, looking at Gina from under his dark, straight eyebrows, then without a word more he left the room.

'What did I say?' Lyn asked, looking after him as he went.

'Oh, nothing ... nothing at all.' Gina kept her eyes down on Byron. 'I'll just drop in the antibiotic powder and do the suturing.

Hold him tightly, Lyn – he is a bit of an acrobat.'

Byron made no attempt to move now as Gina sutured four neat stitches and gave him a final intramuscular injection. 'Good boy, Byron; it didn't hurt a bit, did it?' Adding a temporary patch of gauze to cover the wound, she and Lyn lifted him down to the floor.

'One satisfied customer, at least.' Lyn smiled, and led Byron out to his mistress in the waiting-room.

Gina reflected on Ben's visit, wondering what had prompted him to try to speak to her in the middle of surgery. Was it so important for him to find excuses for last night that he had sent Lyn out of the room deliberately? Had he worried that she was going to misconstrue his action, read more into it than there was?

It was foolish of her, she had already decided, to let her mind dwell on it. She had felt mortified afterwards because of her response and she would just have to get over that embarrassment.

In all conscience, she had no right to feel the way she'd been beginning to feel lately. There was Harriet to think of, her career, the professional relationship she must keep on course between Ben and herself.

But her doubts nagged incessantly. In marked contrast to what she had felt for

Kieron, this sensual awareness that debilitated her yet filled her up with strange new sensations ... the fear and excitement that washed through her when Ben had taken her into his arms and kissed her ... left her with one question in mind, a question she'd thought she would never ask herself, because she had been so certain of her feelings.

Had she ever loved Kieron ... really loved him? Hadn't it been adoration and adulation, emotion usually reserved for the all-perfect male with feet of clay so charmingly hidden and so painfully revealed when fantasy turned to fact?

Kieron had been a wish ... rather than a want.

But when Ben had kissed her, oh, she had wanted that! Wanted it so much that even now she felt the lurching in her stomach that moved swiftly up into her dry throat and into a flash of bright colour on her cheeks as she thought of his lips on her mouth.

Her dismay at her own weakness made her call out sharply to Lyn for her next patient. Work was the only cure for this distressing condition and work she would, so that there was no space left in her mind for the memory of what had happened last night.

CHAPTER SIX

Su-Ling recovered and was discharged, walking without pain – a miracle, as Mrs Timothy had described it – one which Mr Cassell had worked.

Gina was tempted, privately, to agree. The more she saw of Ben's work, the more she was impressed by his skill, his dedication to animals. Why, then was their own relationship so tenuous, when they had so much in common? Perhaps the physical attraction which had flared between them was preventing a deeper working understanding?

Reviewing the situation, Gina reminded herself that Ben had only offered her the job because he was desperate, because Gerald Gorley had let him down at the last moment. Since the beginning, her eagerness and enthusiasm at work had only alienated him. Then, just when things might have been marginally getting better after the evening with Harriet...

Gina sighed deeply. Memory was a precarious travelling companion. Common sense obliterated thought for the most part, but sometimes, when she was near him, when she watched him unobserved...

It was her day off, a Thursday. Ben collided with her coming out of the staffroom mid-morning. The air of coolness between them still lingered and yet, this morning, his grin was spontaneous.

'Thursday? Are you meant to be here?' he asked, the grey eyes drifting over her pale blue jogging-suit.

'I left my car keys here,' she told him, her skin in a light flush under his gaze. 'I was considering a drive over to my parents'.'

'Only considering?' He tilted his dark head, eyebrows raised in a question. 'I wonder … could I interest you in an alternative?'

She frowned. 'What did you have in mind?'

'Purely business,' he answered her casually, the quicksilver eyes alight with good humour. 'We've a client who has a stables near Shaftesbury, Jake Forsythe. One of his mares has a problem with her hock joint… Julian has asked me to take a look before we decide on treatment. I'm shooting out there now.'

'And … you want me … to go with you?'

He shrugged. 'It occurred to me you might appreciate the experience of examining a singularly interesting case, that was all.'

Relaxing a little, she found the offer tempting, but was it a good idea to tempt providence? Not that anything like the other night would ever happen again … but even so…

'I wonder what excuse not to come you're

trying to think up in that lovely head of yours?' He grinned, amused.

'I'm not thinking up any excuse!' she retorted too quickly, then, looking at him from under her dark lashes, she smiled and sighed. 'I haven't really got one, have I?'

He laughed aloud. 'In that case, since Jake's is a fair drive away we'll make a day of it and stop for lunch on the way. And before you say no,' he hurriedly added as she parted her lips to protest, 'come and have a look at the radiographs and see what you think.'

He took her arm and wheeled her into his consulting-room before she knew what was happening. He pulled X-rays from a folder, pinned them up and switched on the light. 'As I say, rather an interesting case.'

Her gaze moved over the outline of the horse's hock joint. To concentrate on it was difficult, she was trying to get over the shock of his invitation and call to mind all her early training in equine practice at the same time. But she managed, quickly absorbed, watching Ben indicate the light and dark areas, her eyes picking out the problem area.

'The horse has been stabled yet she's showing no improvement,' he told her, frowning unhappily. 'So it doesn't seem like an ordinary strain.'

Gina nodded. 'Were these taken very long after the injury?'

'About two weeks, I believe. Julian tried

cold-water bandages first, then cold-hosing over the inflammation, but made little progress, so he decided to take radiographs and here we have the result.'

She looked closer. 'There seems to be some new bone formation. It's not always possible to see the extent of the damage, is it? I mean, whether the articular cartilage is involved or just the soft tissue.'

He glanced at her thoughtfully. 'You're familiar with this type of injury?'

She looked into his curious gaze, realising she would have to explain. 'The junior partner of the Surrey firm I worked for took a particular interest in equine surgery.'

He nodded, pausing, then, without taking his eyes off her, asked, 'Do I know him?'

She shrugged dismissively. 'I shouldn't think so. His name is Kieron Brent.'

'And were horses Kieron Brent's only interest?' he asked sharply.

'What exactly do you mean?' Her mouth tightened as she tried to decide which she resented more – the topic of Kieron Brent or this intrusive line of interrogation.

'I'd have to be an idiot not to sense your reaction while we've been talking,' he persisted, frowning deeply. 'Were you involved with him on a personal level?'

Her jaw dropped in astonishment at his audacity, but she was too shocked to think of an answer and continued to stare at him as his face darkened and he eventually muttered under his breath, 'So ... he's hurt you that much.'

'No...!' Realising he had completely misread her, she shook her head fiercely. 'You've got the wrong idea completely. It's over between–' She stopped, suddenly wondering why she was standing here, her stomach tying in knots, trying to justify herself on a personal issue.

'I thought maybe you'd like to talk about it,' he said slowly with a lazy shrug.

'Horses and hock injuries, yes – but not my private life, which I'm sure would only bore you.' She glanced at her watch. 'I really think I ought to go–'

'Hey!' He held her arm as she moved away. 'So you don't want to talk about Brent; I understand. Fine with me. But don't walk off in a huff ... please?'

He was still holding her arm when they heard the door swing open. Vivienne Armitage gazed back at them, her eyes as cold as ice, flickering over Ben's fingers as they lay on Gina's arm. What was it, Gina wondered on an inner shudder, that she disliked so much about this woman?

'Hello, Viv.' Ben frowned, letting Gina go. 'See you in half an hour, Gina,' he said shortly. 'Wrap up, because there's always a breeze Shaftesbury way.'

'Shaftesbury?' Vivienne stared at him. 'I

hope you're not disappearing... Harvey thinks we have mastitis at the farm again. Could you call out? He's dreadfully worried.'

'Harvey didn't mention it when I saw him on Tuesday,' Ben said in a mystified tone.

Vivienne sighed, smiling sweetly. 'Well, you know how these things flare up.'

Gina could well understand how things 'flared up' – considerably more frequently when Vivienne decided she wanted a larger helping of Ben's attention!

'I'll get Julian to come. I've a call to make with Gina.' Both women stared at him in surprise.

Pink suddenly streaked Vivienne's cheeks, the jealousy in her face transparent. 'Harvey prefers you, Ben; you must know that.'

'I'd better go.' Gina moved towards the door, sensing the atmosphere.

Ben opened the door for her. 'I'll see you in thirty minutes prompt,' he said firmly.

'But Ben!' Viv gasped as Gina hurried out, avoiding the look of shock ill-contained in the other woman's eyes.

She had just sparked off an argument between the two, of that she was sure, she decided as she hurried on her way. Vivienne obviously disliked her and the feeling was mutual, but if it was going to cause scenes like this then she would have to remember to stay well out of the firing line. More complications added to the distinctly sensitive areas of their relationship ... well, it simply would prove intolerable for all concerned.

Just remembering to fetch her keys on the way out, Gina briefly said hello to the girls and hurried on her way, vowing that she would leave for her parents' immediately. Here was one argument Ben wouldn't win and she didn't particularly want to hang around to hear his excuses.

But, caught by curiosity and a perverse hope that Viv Armitage wouldn't win the day, Gina hovered in her front room. From the bay window she could see her car parked outside the surgery.

As time wore on it seemed her instincts were right. The blue car remained where it was. She changed into black leggings shaped to the contours of her long legs, a cerise sweater with a huge roll-neck and casual boots. If she visited her parents no doubt she would take a walk with her mother through the hills and over to Corfe. She would need to be well wrapped-up, even though the sun was blistering through the clouds.

The knock at the door made her jump.

When she opened it, Ben was dressed in a casual sweater too, a grey one which matched the colour of his eyes. 'Very appropriate!' His gaze wandered over her slim figure and lingered. 'You look great. Are you ready?'

'But ... what about ... Vivienne?' she asked in surprise.

He shrugged. 'What about her? Julian can go.'

Gina looked for the evidence of Viv's car over his shoulder and found none.

'Well? What are we waiting for?' he demanded with a grin and, before long, she found herself sitting in the Discovery, heading towards the hills of Wiltshire, a compact disc playing light classical music and an expression on Ben's face she couldn't quite work out. What had happened between the two lovers? she wondered. Why hadn't Viv got her way?

Gina sat back and thought. She simply did not care. It was a beautiful day. She was going to enjoy herself ... which was, she reflected wryly, more than Vivienne Armitage was doing right now!

'Jake's both a friend and a client of Julian's,' Ben explained as they travelled. 'Known each other for years. Jake dabbles with thoroughbreds as a hobby but he takes it very seriously.'

Gina looked surprised. 'Rather an expensive hobby!'

'Jake went into property speculation in the early eighties and hasn't looked back. Chamois is a favourite, a self-indulgence, he says. She's four ... plenty of racing potential, so naturally he's pretty keen to get her well again.'

'How did the injury occur?'

'Early morning exercise. She came back lame, so Julian's been treating her with phenylbutazone and ultrasound. A support bandage seemed to help for a while, and she's had plenty of box rest, but apparently the hock is very swollen.'

'Severe injuries can take months of rest, though,' Gina added with a frown.

'Hmm.' Ben nodded. 'Jake's not a particularly patient man. He's had injuries to his horses before but he's had a lucky streak and they've all cleared up relatively quickly. This is his first major disaster.'

As they came to a brow of a hill, Gina gave a gasp, the countryside was so stunning below them. It was hard to believe that these very fields had been covered in snow only a week ago – the weather had improved so much since. The road, a ribbon of slippery grey, wound through the valley.

'Beautiful, isn't it?' Ben said. Then, shifting gear as they began the descent, he asked, 'Hungry?'

She was beginning to feel hungry. Having intended to eat a late breakfast before her day began, she had sufficed with orange juice and toast. 'Ravenous!' She smiled and, as she looked at him, was aware that the day had opened out, free from tension, his face relaxed as the sunshine lit up their spirits and the beautiful countryside at the same time.

Lovers Crossed was set in the valley. Rustic

benches and tables outside welcomed travellers and the smell of food tempted from inside. The meal was simple but delicious – scampi served in baskets. They drank Perrier with ice and lemon and Ben watched her with wry amusement as she finished every scrap.

'It's refreshing to see an appetite in a woman,' he observed with a grin. 'Just think, you would have missed all this if you hadn't come today.'

Sipping her drink, she looked at him through thoughtful violet eyes. 'I wasn't sure the arrangement stood.'

'You mean that business with Viv?' He shrugged dismissively. 'Julian will cope. Viv will cool down.'

'Will she? You must know her very well!'

He looked at her with fresh interest. 'You don't like Viv, do you?'

'I haven't formed an opinion,' she answered stiffly, realising he had caught the wariness in her tone.

'Ah! You're exercising a woman's prerogative to defer judgement, I see,' he teased, grey eyes sparkling.

She hesitated at his mockery. 'I hardly think I have a right to judge.'

'Then why do I get the impression you really could say a lot more than you're letting on?' he pressed lightly.

'It's not my business to comment, Ben,

just as–'

'Brent isn't mine?'

'You're determined not to give up on the subject, aren't you?' She sighed.

'Is there any reason why I should? If there is, tell me and we won't mention him again.'

No, there was no reason why they should not discuss Kieron Brent, Gina reflected as she studied the deceiving grey warmth of those heavy-lidded, languorous eyes. Once upon a time, yes, even mentioning Kieron's name would have been painful, but her life had changed so much! As a woman she had matured after the accident, fighting to get back on her feet, just to walk again, take a few steps away from the wheelchair and then the crutches. She would never forget her first day in the physiotherapy gym when she had let go of those crutches and hobbled ... literally hobbled a couple of feet towards her physiotherapist. Perhaps it was then that, symbolically, she had thrown away the crutches of her emotional ties ... those to Kieron, such as they were. Six months blending into a year without seeing the face you needed to see so badly ...yes, in those first clumsy steps she had taken, she had come to terms with rejection and set her course towards a new life. And then this man had come along. A man who had offered her the chance to start again ... and, with it, awoken a sleeping tiger inside her...

'We can talk about Kieron if you like, Ben,' she said indifferently, her cheeks dark with fresh colour, 'but I think the subject would probably bore you to tears.'

'Why not let me be the judge of that?' he suggested.

She hesitated. It had been a long time since she opened her heart. 'I first met Kieron during my last year qualifying,' she managed after a moment's hesitation. 'When his firm took me on after my finals we seemed to have a lot in common. We both loved the theatre. Sometimes we'd have dinner in the West End or go to a show.' She gave a rueful smile. 'At first, we tried to be discreet about going out together, but, of course, when you're living in a close-knit community discretion rarely is successful.'

'Was discretion really necessary?' he asked, leaning back in his chair.

She shrugged. 'Neither of us wanted to encourage gossip. But, as time went by, it seemed impractical to deliberately hide the fact that we were seeing one another.'

'Just ... seeing one another?' Ben asked doubtfully.

She gave a small sigh, looking at him from under her dark lashes. 'We discussed marriage, it's true. But, well, I suppose I'm rather old-fashioned. I wanted what I had grown up with, the kind of affinity my parents share with one another. Marriage always meant a great deal to them and so it did to me. I'm not sure Kieron viewed our relationship or marriage in the same way; he looked at it more objectively, more practically than I.'

'Marriage is a way of life,' Ben murmured, his eyes steady on her face.

'For some people,' Gina agreed. 'But not for others. It was hardly fair of me to thrust my point of view on Kieron...'

'Or for him to expect you to change?'

She nodded. 'Our difference of opinion became a problem. In fact we'd been arguing the night we drove home from the city after a show.' Her eyes went up to meet Ben's steady gaze. 'Weather conditions were bad, fog and ice. The car hit a patch...' She shook her head, shuddering at the memory. 'Kieron fighting with the wheel is the last thing I remember.'

'Was he injured too?'

'Shock mostly, and cuts and bruising.'

'So he was discharged and you were flat on your back?'

'He came to see me!' she defended automatically at Ben's tone. 'We talked about the change in our circumstances, decided to stop seeing one another. There was the difficulty of getting to the hospital with such a demanding schedule. He had his future to think of,' she added hastily, not really knowing why she was still avoiding the truth, though in her heart she knew Kieron had been unable to accept the responsibility of a virtual cripple in his life.

'And you didn't?' Ben persisted.

'Yes … well, no… I couldn't expect him to wait around for months when I didn't even know myself if…' She fumbled for words. 'Kieron was a junior partner in the firm; he carried a lot of responsibility…'

Ben sat there studying her, the deep grey eyes resting on her face. Her heart raced. 'I'm sorry.' She laughed nervously. 'I haven't stopped talking.'

'I think you rather needed to get it off your chest,' he said evenly. 'Are you still in love with him?'

She drew in her breath sharply, shocked at his question. Suddenly the picture of Kieron's angry face flashed through her mind, and the quarrel they'd had that night. She had held out against the growing urgency of his lovemaking, the real cause of their conflict. Was that why he had been driving so fast – out of anger and frustration?

'I shouldn't have asked,' Ben muttered, mistaking her preoccupation for reticence. Broodingly he frowned across the table. 'I would offer to bore you with the Cassell family saga, only Harry's rather beaten me to it, hasn't she?'

They both smiled, the tension easing as coffee arrived. They discussed the theatre and books and sailing and, when he glanced at his watch and frowned, it was with disappointment that she heard him remark, 'Time, I think, for us to be going. A pity ... we've managed not to quarrel for two whole hours.'

In the cold air outside, she felt his hand gently slip to the small of her back and steer her to the Discovery. It was only a touch but inside it seemed as if her bones were melting. She shrugged the sensation away. Today they had talked as individuals, not professionals ... and, as long as she was always vigilant, what harm was there in that?

Several inches shorter than Ben, Jake Forsythe was around fortyish, with bright blue eyes and brown wavy hair. He clenched her small hand in his as she sampled the unswerving gaze of a well-seasoned Lothario.

'You old rascal, Ben Cassell, no wonder you've been keeping her under wraps!' he complimented flamboyantly. 'Shall we have drinks first?' They stood in the courtyard of a Tudor manor-house. To reach it they had driven along narrow, almost impassable country lanes, reaching the sedate building at the end of a wide gravel sweep. She heard the clink of hooves on cobbles and knew the stables couldn't be far away.

'Not if I know your drinks, Jake.' Ben grinned. 'And we've just had lunch, thanks.'

'Later, then,' Jake whispered flirtatiously to Gina. 'Chamois is in her box, of course, where she has been for several weeks.' He led them through an archway to the back of the manor and into the stables' courtyard where horses were being groomed and turned out.

Chamois was an elegant chestnut thoroughbred. She had a long neck and proud head and she nibbled at the hay basket, her large brown eyes watchful of the visitors to her box.

'She's usually even-tempered,' Jake told them, smoothing a hand over the sweep of glossy withers. 'But the leg is upsetting her. Julian has done what he can and the anti-inflammatory drugs relieve her pain, but, Ben, I'm beginning to despair. Just look at that hock joint.'

Gina could see at a glance that the swelling was incredibly ugly and must be painful. Ben walked forward and gently stroked the horse, getting to know her. She turned her head and nudged him, but stood quite still. After a while he bent down to get a closer look.

'The swelling is worst on the inside and the front of the hock, isn't it?' he murmured.

'It started to go down a bit after the cold-water bandages, but it was only temporary.' Jake stood anxiously watching.

Ben was quiet, his fingers gently probing the area, travelling down to the cannon and back up to the hamstring. 'There's an awful lot of heat around the joint.' He sighed.

Jake nodded miserably. 'And it doesn't

look any better than it was when she did it.'

'It's the swelling,' Ben explained. 'The excess synovial fluid. If collateral ligaments are sprained, then the swelling is even worse around the joint. Flexing it causes pain and the injury is only accentuated by any manipulation. Gina, do you want to come and have a look?'

Eager to examine Chamois, she moved forward. The mare allowed her to feel around the swollen hock, and Gina's suspicion that the injury was going to take a long while to clear up grew; Jake Forsythe was not going to see any quick results.

When she had finished, they walked out into daylight and Jake frowned. 'What's the worst?'

'You have to remember that it isn't always absolutely clear whether the articular cartilage is involved in this sort of damage and I may be wrong,' Ben said with a shrug.

'You aren't normally,' Jake grinned wryly. 'Go on.'

'Well, personally, I think there is articular cartilage damage. To be frank, my long-term prognosis is guarded – and it isn't what you want to hear – she'll need at least another couple more months of complete rest and after that just gentle exercise.'

'No racing this year?' Jake groaned.

'Unlikely. Gina? What do you think?'

She looked at Jake with sympathy. 'I'm

afraid I have to agree. But Ben ... isn't there a drug now, unfortunately an expensive one, which can be given to help recovery? It's been tested and successfully used for the treatment of acute joint disorders, hasn't it?'

'You mean sodium hyaluronate?'

'What's that?' Jake intercepted, looking brighter.

'Don't build up your hopes,' Ben warned. 'But Gina's right. Sodium hyaluronate is a drug administered into the joint which sometimes ... sometimes, I emphasise ... permits a more rapid return to normal function. But it's a gamble and to be perfectly honest I don't think even if it was successful you'd be wise to race her this year.'

'But does it ease the pain?' Jake asked.

'In a lot of cases.'

'Let's talk in the house,' Jake decided and they followed him through a stirring breeze across the courtyard to the house.

For the next hour the topic of conversation was horses. Jake took them into his library where he drank an aperitif and they sipped on Darjeeling tea. Gina liked the atmosphere of the old room spilling over with books.

Having decided to treat Chamois with a course of sodium hyaluronate, Jake showed them over the manor, along carved wooden balconies and picture-lined galleries. Most of the oils were of horses. Two ex-wives and a rather dubious number of offspring had led him to the conclusion that horses were less troublesome than people.

When they eventually left, the Discovery's lights blazed along the lanes as a gloom began to spread over the countryside.

'He's a character, isn't he?' Ben grinned. 'What did you think of Chamois?'

Gina watched the large brown hands turn the wheel and they were at last on the main road. 'She's beautiful. But I think even with the drug she'll need a long lay-up.'

They drove on in amiable silence. She had been impressed by Ben's quiet, confident knowledge, his unassuming manner with Jake. By comparison Kieron loved to be at the centre of things, at the heart of what was going on in the practice, quick to use new methods and drugs. Ben's careful approach to the treatment of Chamois was a startling change. Or was it, she thought, with sudden clarity, she who had changed in her perception of people? She had stood in real awe of Kieron at times. But she had never really seen him as a person, never really looked beyond the person she had thrust on him – and which, in all fairness, he did not deserve.

The homeward journey almost over, Ben slowed down, making a small noise of irritation. 'I've forgotten the wine,' he groaned. 'Harry's cooking a special meal tonight. Not that it really matters. We probably wouldn't finish a bottle between us anyway.'

'A special meal?' Gina asked, curious.

He grinned wryly. 'My birthday. To be honest, it completely slipped my mind.'

It was characteristic, she thought with acute sympathy for Harriet. How did a man become so wrapped up with his work, he could even manage to forget his own birthday? No wonder Harriet was rebelling! Between Viv Armitage and the practice the poor girl stood little chance!

'I may have some pretty innocuous supermarket vino in the fridge.' She smiled. 'You're welcome to it if it saves you a journey back into town – and Harriet won't think you've forgotten then.'

He grinned, turning the Discovery into the lane. 'You women always stick together, don't you?'

'Does it show?' And, laughing, she added softly, 'Many happy returns, Ben.'

He stared at her, half smiling. 'Do you know, that's the nicest thing you've said to me all day?'

Her face flushed and her eyes darkened as large white teeth appeared teasingly behind parted lips and he added, 'So ... do I deserve a birthday kiss?'

Gina felt her throat go dry and a small tremble quiver down her backbone; she told herself firmly that there was no smouldering chemistry going on in those unnerving grey eyes.

Luckily the bright lights of the practice signalled their journey's end.

Had not Stuart been hurrying across the car park and stopped to change direction towards them, she had the strongest suspicion that Ben would have jerked the Discovery to a halt and claimed her answer.

CHAPTER SEVEN

'Road-traffic accident!' Stuart told them hurriedly as they climbed out. 'A stray, by the sound of it. No one's claiming ownership but a woman was good enough to phone.' He tilted his head towards the surgery and added with a wry smile, 'Be prepared for bedlam! It's been one of those days!'

The teasing suggestion of the kiss was forgotten in the panic as Gina hurried as fast as she could, trying to keep up with Ben's long strides into Reception.

Vicki stood behind the desk looking fraught. 'Thank goodness you're back, Ben! It's been chaos. The last of the afternoon's open surgery has only just left and then there's Mrs Eldridge. She phoned in to say her pregnant Cavalier King Charles is in labour and making awful whining noises.'

Ben thrust a large hand through his hair. 'It would be tonight of all nights, wouldn't it? Are they bringing her in?'

'Mrs Eldridge says her husband's out and she hasn't got the car.'

'I'll have to attend the dog.' He sighed. 'She brought the bitch in earlier this week, thinking she was beginning labour. The woman was almost having an anxiety attack herself.'

'I'll do the visit,' Gina suggested immediately. 'I'll just go to the dispensary and–'

Ben laid a restraining hand on her arm, shaking his head. 'Mrs Eldridge won't see anyone else.'

'She's a rather difficult lady, to put it mildly,' Vicki agreed warningly. 'She specified you, Ben.'

'But surely on this occasion...?' Gina's voice faded as her employer frowned, his eyes reflecting the inner struggle she knew must be going on behind them. Her heart went out to him. Trying to balance family life and a demanding career took its toll and she was filled with a sudden and unnerving compassion which prompted her to give a tremulous smile. 'Then I suppose I'd better go and see Harriet and try to explain on your behalf?'

'I'd be very grateful.' His eyes lingered, his large hand remaining on her arm, his body warmth permeating through to her skin, and she swallowed hard, trying to disguise her embarrassment in front of Vicki.

But if Vicki registered the intimacy between them, she showed no sign of it after Ben's disappearance as she sank into a chair. 'Poor Harry! No wonder she doesn't like animals. She's always having to take second place to them. And without a mother it must be worse. From what Audrey told me, Sarah was just as much a dedicated vet as Ben. The kid's always taken a back seat. Her grand-mother tried to make up for it, I think.'

It was, sadly, true, Gina reflected silently. Ben must know it in his heart of hearts. But he was a proud and private man, his daughter equally so, made from the same mould. If only they would talk … really talk with one another!

'We used to go and have coffee in our breaks with Audrey,' Vicki continued. 'She was very sweet, always ready to listen to our problems. From what she told me I gather after Sarah's death they made a fresh start of it by coming here rather than staying in Truro.'

Avoiding joining in with Vicki's well-mean-ing but somewhat dangerous observations, remembering how Harriet had learned some painful truths, Gina gathered her things together. 'I'd better go across, Vicki. Nothing else outstanding, is there?'

'Only checking the lists for tomorrow.' Vicki glanced at the appointment book. 'But they can wait.'

Harriet stood at the window as Gina walked through the wicket gate, her slender shape silhouetted against the bright light of the drawing-room.

She opened the door dressed in a lilac blouson top and a mini-skirt with black tights and dainty pumps. Around her neck she wore a silver locket and studs of silver in her ears.

146

'Oh, Harriet, you look lovely!' Gina exclaimed, but, to her dismay, tears sprang up in the blue eyes.

'He's not coming, is he?' Harriet asked, biting them back.

'Your father had an emergency call. Let me explain–'

But the girl turned, hurrying into the hall. Gina saw the quick movement, a hand brushed across a wet cheek, as Harriet ran to the stairs and leapt them, two at a time. Gina heard a door slam upstairs, her nerves jumping with it.

Silence engulfed the house. The night air swept in and curled around her face. She was tempted to walk out into it, the conflict in this family running too deep for a few consoling words to ease. Perhaps it was better to let Harriet get over her anger and maybe by the time Ben got home...

But she couldn't go; her conscience wouldn't let her. With one ear on the stairs, she hung up her coat, went into the kitchen and prepared two mugs of tea. Had Harriet locked herself in her room? She'd done that often enough herself in her teens!

Upstairs, Gina stopped at the only door along the landing which was closed, all the others leading off to darkened bedrooms. 'Harriet? May I come in?'

After a while she tried again. 'Harriet?'

Slowly the door opened and Harriet's

crumpled face emerged.

'I'll go away if you like,' Gina said quickly. 'I don't want to be a nuisance if you would rather be alone.' She handed her the tea, glancing into the bedroom, a typical mixture of adolescence and maturity. Pop-group posters, a desk and word processor, a glass mobile hanging over a threadbare teddy sitting drunkenly on a chest.

'I'm ... I'm sorry I was rude,' Harriet apologised.

'Would you like to talk?'

Harriet shrugged, her face sullen. 'I didn't mean to take it out on you. I suppose he's gone to Vivienne's?'

So that was what was going through her mind! Gina shook her head but, before she could speak, Harriet blurted out, 'If Mummy were alive he wouldn't look twice at Vivienne. Mummy was much more beautiful and very clever!'

The words hit Gina like a physical blow. It was a few moments before she could regain her composure, but when she did Harriet was quietly sobbing. Gina slipped an arm around her shoulders and to her relief she wasn't rebuffed. 'I know, Harriet. Your mother was clever and dedicated ... and exceptionally beautiful, just like you.'

Harriet stared up through puffy eyes. 'How do you know?'

Gina admitted to discovering the snaps.

148

Harriet sniffed, brought out a tissue and blew her nose. 'But Nana says my nature's like Daddy's,' she mumbled guilelessly.

'Yes, you're a very earnest young woman. And very sensitive ... like your father, though he doesn't like to show it. And, incidentally, on the subject of your father; he's gone to attend a pregnant bitch. Otherwise he would have been home here, diving into that meal he was telling me about.'

'Really?' Harriet grinned, wiping her red cheeks. 'Are you hungry? I've prepared stacks of food: homemade vegetable soup, spaghetti carbonara and apple pie with cream and ice-cream.'

Gina reflected, as she followed Harriet downstairs and into the kitchen and helped her serve the delicious meal which she had reluctantly agreed to eat in Ben's place, that perhaps the day wasn't going to end so badly after all. She felt closer to Harriet, so much so that she had no difficulty in telling her, as they ate, of her own similar experiences as a teenager.

'My parents were in business,' she divulged easily, 'and Mum had to divide her time between me and helping Dad. Sometimes, I hated their fashion business and all its demands.'

'At least your father wasn't always at the beck and call of animals as well as people,' Harriet observed drily.

Gina realised that Harriet's dislike of animals wasn't actually focused on animals themselves but on her parents' dedication to their careers. 'People in the fashion world were far worse,' Gina reproved gently. 'Dad was always going away to shows and exhibitions. I resented it until I began to see what a good life I was having because of it. A lot of my friends' families couldn't afford to send them on to further education. Mine could. I was able to become a vet–'

'But I don't want to be a vet!' Harriet sighed, harpooning the last mouthful of pasta. 'Why should I do science A levels if I don't want to?'

'Perhaps your father wants you to do them because you shine at them and it would be a valuable gift to waste if you didn't,' Gina suggested reasonably. 'Have you ever tried discussing your true feelings with him?'

Harriet slumped in her chair, chewing on her bottom lip. Obviously she hadn't. But how was she to convince Harriet to talk to Ben – especially after tonight?

With the three courses demolished Gina sat with Harriet by the log fire. The conversation turned to Harriet's mother and Gina listened quietly, forming a firmer picture of Sarah through Harriet's eyes. The predominant impression was of a young, talented and beautiful woman who loved her daughter, but who also loved her work, sometimes to the extent of inflaming Harriet's desire to challenge it.

Gina's attention slipped to the kittens as they lay in the teenager's lap. Perhaps through the kittens Harriet was learning to come to terms with her true feelings for animals.

The tired girl yawned. 'If you want to go to bed, Harriet, I'll wait for your father,' Gina offered, wondering what complication could have set in with the King Charles to keep him so long.

'Oh, you needn't bother!' She gathered the kittens in her arms and peered out of the window. 'I'm fine by myself.'

Gina resisted the urge to disagree. Harriet was far too wound up to be left alone. 'I'll make a hot drink ... and, by the time we've finished it, I expect he'll be home.'

Gina ached for bed. But she had no intention of leaving until Ben came home. Harriet disappeared to return the kittens to their bed and Gina leaned back, watching the flames crawl into the chimney, aware of the rhythmic ticking of the grandfather clock in the hall.

It was with a jolt that she suddenly awoke, the house in stillness. She slipped up the stairs quietly, going along to the bedroom on tiptoes. Harriet lay on the bed in a cotton nightshirt, sound asleep.

Greatly relieved that there would be no

confrontation tonight with Ben, she turned off the bedside light and drew up the duvet. Harriet's face was innocently childlike in slumber and a pang of sympathy touched her heart as she realised how fond she was becoming of the girl.

Creeping down the stairs, she stopped still. Keys turned in the lock and Ben walked in, coat collar turned up against the cold, his cheeks hollowed and his forehead deeply creased as he stared at her.

The grey eyes travelled up the stairs anxiously.

'Harriet's asleep,' she whispered, smiling, and he followed her into the drawing-room.

Closing the door quietly, he threw his coat over the back of the sofa. The grey of his sweater seemed to emphasise the deep grey of his eyes, dark blue smudges of tiredness just beneath them. 'How did it go?' he asked tensely.

'She understood, I think. But I'm afraid you missed a marvellous meal.'

'She's forgiven me?' he asked grimly.

'I wouldn't go as far as to say that ... but she'll feel better in the morning. What happened with the King Charles?'

'A complicated birth.' He sighed, running a large hand through the dark hair. 'There were only two but the first one was a plump little chap ... he was what all the straining was about and I had to give him some assistance. The second was a small bitch and came out easily.' He laughed lightly. 'Mrs Eldridge had problems, though. The birth brought on a "spasm", as she called it. Luckily her husband arrived home just in time to find the smelling-salts.'

Gina laughed too, watching Ben's face smooth out as he relaxed. He walked closer, saying softly, 'I don't know what I would have done without your help tonight. I was in a heck of a fix. I've let poor Harry down before and the blessed thing is, it always seems to happen on special occasions. Was she terribly upset?'

'It took some while for her to come around,' she answered guardedly. 'I ... I think she really does feel left out at times.'

'Did she say that?'

'Not in so many words ... but subconsciously I think she's been trying to draw your attention–'

'But why talk to you?' he broke in sharply. 'Why not me?'

Gina recognised dangerous ground when she was on it and by the look of Ben's face she had overstepped the mark.

'Maybe because we're both the same sex and both only children,' she tried, aiming to defuse the tension. 'Maybe tonight she simply needed someone to listen to her and I just happened to be here.'

He walked to the window, broad shoulders

stiff, frowning out into the dark. 'Damn it!' he cursed under his breath.

Gina was silent. Here she was, piggy in the middle, understanding the conflict only too well, yet unable to help because she might alienate him even more.

'Tonight I felt I couldn't just walk in and make a few pathetic excuses.' She sighed frustratedly. 'Harriet wouldn't have wanted to be patronised and she needed a listening ear. It would, of course, have been better if it were yours,' she added tactfully, only to find his face intensely angry as he swivelled around, fiery grey eyes narrowed at her.

'So what do you suggest I should do? Give up being a vet and play at housemother?' he growled.

'No … of course not!' she almost shouted back, all but giving in to the urge to lose her temper. 'Talk to her, Ben! Just find time soon to talk to her. Persevere, even if she doesn't respond at first. She loves you – deeply. She just needs reassurance and your understanding…'

Suddenly aware of those cool grey eyes warming and the sharp, masculine contours of his strong face softening, she came to a breathless halt. The thick coppery hair curled down on to his collar and some crazy impulse made her want to run her hands through it, to smooth her fingers into its thickness, her anger bewilderingly changing into a strong

154

physical desire to be swept into his arms.

'I ... I really must be going,' she said thickly, feeling dizzy, as he reached out towards her, firm fingers wrapping around her arms.

'Don't go. Stay...' he whispered huskily.

She shook her head, the pounding of her heart beating heavily like a drum under her ribs. His grey eyes glinted as they passed over her face, the irises turning from deep grey to blue-grey as she stared into them. He couldn't be going to kiss her, could he? Surely they both knew this mustn't happen!

When his lips touched hers, the world spun. She wanted to reach out and steady it, but her hands were clasping his strong arms, the feel of muscle hardening beneath her fingertips, and she groaned under another hectic wave of desire. Her mouth quivered as she allowed herself to give in to his passionate lips prising hers open, overwhelmed by his stark masculinity, dazed and drowning in a sea of pleasure.

The fierce desire which seemed to crash between their bodies made her melt and shiver at the same time, her breasts stinging with sensual excitement in instant response to the way his strong arms crushed her to him. Her hoarse cry of abandoned desire was swept away on deep wave of erotic sensation as his kiss grew deeper and deeper, a sense of unreality swamping her dazed brain.

'Oh, God, Gina!' he whispered as, for a moment, his lips parted from hers, his voice alerting her mind to some kind of common sense as she flattened her trembling hands against his chest.

Her face flamed as she stared up at him, her body pulsing with hot blood. 'Th-this is madness, Ben!'

His fingers trapped her to him. 'Why is it madness?'

She pulled away harder and this time he let her go as they faced each other, her mouth stinging with the touch of his passionate kiss.

His face tightened, mouth in a hard line at her stricken silence. 'Good grief, Gina ... do you think I planned kissing you like that? Heavens above, I kissed you because I couldn't help myself!'

She tried to pull herself together, her thudding heart almost drowning his words. 'Ben ... can't you see the dangers? The complications of–'

'Complications?' he repeated angrily, his mouth white. 'Damn the bloody complications!'

The telephone shrilled into the silence, a distorted echo of his angry words. He turned impatiently and went to answer it, striding across the room, broad shoulders tensed.

'Thanks,' she heard him say after a few minutes. 'I'm busy now but I'll pick it up tomorrow.'

'That was Viv,' he was forced to explain as he faced her. 'The Eldridge place was only half a mile down the road from the Armitage farm; I called in on my way home tonight. I seem to have left my stethoscope there.'

Gina couldn't believe her ears! While she had been here comforting his daughter, trying to solve the problems he should have been solving, going through agony trying to sort them out on his behalf, he had been with his mistress! Too angry to speak, she headed for the door.

'Gina!' He blocked her way. 'Don't go like this. I'm sorry about tonight ... it won't happen again.'

No, it will never happen again! Gina promised herself, not trusting herself to utter another word. In the hall he caught up with her as she reached for her coat. 'What the hell is going on? I've apologised. You can't condemn a man for a kiss.'

'I'm not condemning you,' she answered coolly, erupting inside with fury. 'Goodnight, Ben.'

She felt quite sick when she got in, standing in the darkness. She tried to assemble her thoughts but it was no use. His touch, his kiss, the way he felt warred with the evidence she had discovered that he was using her, even though he might not consciously be aware of it.

Her introspection endured until the early

hours, a torment so intense, she hadn't realised she was capable of so deep a feeling. Under the anger, the tide of emotion which swept her feelings into furore – there was more.

Jealousy had stolen its insidious way into her life.

It wasn't until the following afternoon in the dispensary that she saw him again. He was storing vaccines in the refrigerator as she went in. Too late to retreat, Gina moved towards the cupboard where the drug she needed was kept.

'Gina…?' His voice was cool and calm, as she expected it to be, so different from the way she was feeling inside, but she reminded herself firmly that it was he who'd made the mistake of trying to use her and it was a mistake she would not allow him to make again.

'This isn't the time or place to bring it up, but last night… I'm afraid I misread you completely.'

'Misread?' Her violet eyes darkened as she turned towards him.

'Yes.' His eyes guardedly flicked over her face as though trying to read her emotions. 'I thought you–'

'Whatever you thought, you thought wrongly,' she corrected him. 'You gave me a chance when you took me on as a locum, Ben, and I'm grateful. I hope I can show my

158

gratitude in the standard of my work … but I won't – and I emphasise this – I won't be drawn into an affair with you.'

'An affair?' He drew himself up, his grey eyes hard as he gave a choked laugh. 'What is your definition of an affair?'

'It's nothing I would choose to discuss with you,' she answered shortly.

For a moment she felt a surge of satisfaction in seeing his expression. But her satisfaction was short-lived as he shrugged and moved away with his broad back to her. 'If that's the way you want it,' he muttered, turning back to stare, his eyes fixed on her with that look she had come to know so well as part of the professional mask.

Tensely she reached out for the drug she wanted. Seeing but not seeing, her gaze flicked along the top row of shelving.

'Can I help?' he asked coolly, seeing her hesitation.

She shook her head. 'I've a young dog with suspected enteritis, that's all.' Fortunately she found the antibiotic, slipped it into her coat pocket and closed the cupboard doors.

Together, in silence, they left the room. 'Oh … did you retrieve your stethoscope?' she asked in a cool voice before they parted.

He looked at her blankly. 'My stethoscope … oh, I'd forgotten. No. Stuart's passing that way today. I'll ask him to pick it up for me.'

Startled by the answer, which was not what

she expected, she left. As she walked into her consulting-room she couldn't understand his reaction. Surely the stethoscope was an ideal excuse to see Vivienne?

Drawing her mind back to work, she began to examine the dog who had been brought in with vomiting and diarrhoea.

'He's dehydrated,' Gina explained to the young woman who had bought the dog on impulse. She had not checked his breeding and the poor condition he was in had slowly deteriorated over two weeks. 'I'm going to treat him with fluid therapy ... if needs be, put him on an intravenous drip. I can only do that here, so he'll have to stay, I'm afraid.'

In the special unit of the recovery-room, Bev helped Gina to settle him into a warm cage. 'Enteritis is a horrible germ, isn't it?' Bev sighed.

'It's nasty, but, thank goodness, treatable,' Gina nodded. 'The trouble is, it's so easily transmissible between dogs. Pups and young dogs are the most vulnerable, so we'll take a stool specimen and keep him to small amounts of fluid today. I'll put him on the drip if he doesn't respond.'

Bev left and Gina watched the thin little body of the mongrel. His head looked too big for his body, his light brown coat fitting his ribs and his haunches like a glove. If he didn't improve by tomorrow morning she would have to fit the drip.

Pressing on with the afternoon, she spent her next hour in theatre. The female tortoiseshell cat drifted off immediately as Bev administered the anaesthetic. Gina made the first swift incision in the left side, cutting through muscle to discover the uterus. The procedure took her less than five minutes, though she really had no need to time herself. But, after being out of practice for so long, she extracted a personal goal of swiftness and efficiency from herself.

Bev was a good nurse, premeditating all her movements, and the ops Gina had performed with Stuart had certainly refreshed her memory from training. Now she was doing them almost without thinking. Finding the ovaries and clamping the artery, she tied the ligature, her eyes sweeping up to meet Bev's admiring gaze.

'Brilliant.' Bev grinned. 'You're really quick now. You'd never believe you'd been off for so long.'

Gina felt a warm glow; yes, it was wonderful to have her confidence back. She really did feel able to tackle anything surgically. Surgically, she impressed on herself, thinking of Harriet and Ben ... she would steer clear of the emotional minefields, though!

When she had severed the uterus, she deftly inserted a suture through the layers of muscle. 'Almost finished.' She smiled. 'Just the injection of antibiotic and the closing up. This evening she'll need watching carefully, though; so will my little mongrel.'

'No problem, I'm staying on,' Bev told her as they lifted the cat into a recovery cage. 'If you let me know what fluid he must have – and there are a couple of Stuart's cases in … a full house, actually.'

'Poor you,' Gina sympathised.

'I love it,' Bev said with a bright smile. 'I wouldn't be doing anything special tonight anyway. I'd much prefer to be with the animals than watching TV.'

'What about your boyfriend; doesn't he mind?' Gina asked curiously.

'No such luck at the moment.' Bev sighed. 'We broke up last week.' Then she laughed bitterly. 'He said I should marry a vet, would you believe?'

Gina frowned. 'There's two ways of looking at marrying into the profession … it depends how much you love the work, I think.'

'If I could find an older man, I'd be happy enough,' Bev said with startling honesty. 'The young ones just don't seem to be on my wavelength. They get jealous because I'm crazy over animals.'

Gina refrained from saying that jealousy wasn't exclusive to younger men! Her own recent experience had made her cautious of passing any advice, least of all on the subject of falling in love. Relieved that there were two cases of skin infection waiting to be seen, she managed to avoid further discussion on the subject.

Gina saw the first dog, a German shepherd, and abraded a small section of skin surface with a scalpel and set aside the specimen on the blade for microscopic examination. The four-year-old was a particularly bad case, his long-haired coat displaying large patches of infected skin made worse by self-mutilation.

'I'm afraid it's a condition we call sarcoptic mange,' she explained to the bewildered owner. 'It's contagious, so I'm going to recommend a dip for you to bathe him in. The Prolate has to be mixed with water, very carefully, because it's very strong.'

'What exactly is sarcoptic mange?' the young man asked.

Gina displayed an area under her gloved hands. 'If you look closely you'll see it's a parasite which affects the outer layers of skin, probably picked up while you were out walking with him either from another infected dog or perhaps a fox. And just here...' She moved her finger to point at a small grey bean-shaped parasite attached to the skin of the Alsatian. 'Here is a tick, too. These are more of a nuisance than painful.'

'Can you take it out?'

She shook her head. 'No, not yet. After you have used the Prolate, we can remove it then.'

'Wouldn't it come off now?'

'It might, but it isn't advisable. Ticks are

blood-sucking parasites and if pulled away sometimes the mouth parts are left embedded in the skin and these lead to infection. So it's wise only to remove them once they have been destroyed. If you'll bring him back in when you've used the full course of treatment I'll remove any ticks for you.'

Occasionally, in between clients, Gina found her mind wandering back to her conversation with Bev and, inevitably, to Ben. If he was the compassionate and caring person he was with animals, how could he be so insensitive with her? Was his attitude retaliation, she wondered, against being dealt such an unfair blow with the death of his wife?

Gina found herself staring at a rough collie dog, sitting beside the small figure of a young boy.

'Damian thinks there's something embedded in the ear... Basil's head has been lop-sided, with one ear lower than the other,' Bev explained and hurried out into the passageway as Stuart called her.

The boy had a face full of freckles and greenish eyes to match his lovely red hair. Gina smiled and knelt down to stroke the collie.

'So how long has he been like this?' she asked Damian.

'A few weeks. Mum said she thinks Basil's got something stuck in it.'

Gina lifted up the flap of Basil's ear. It was

clean enough, but possibly the problem lay deeper in the ear canal. 'Hold him still, Damian,' she warned, 'because I'll have to take a look.'

The boy squatted on the floor, patting his knees. The dog lay down, rolled over and rested his head on the youngster's knees. Damian grinned. 'He thinks he's ET. You know, when ET nearly died? Bas can do a lot of tricks. We watch the telly and copy them.'

Gina laughed. 'You might be on television yourselves at this rate.'

Looking down her auroscope into the dog's ear canal, she searched for the tiny white dots she expected to find, which were ear mites, a common cause of trouble. 'Has Basil had any discharge from the ear, have you noticed?' she asked when she couldn't discover any.

The boy shook his head. 'No ... but he scratches it a lot and shakes his head. What are those things?'

Gina inserted forceps gently inside the ear. 'They're called forceps... I shan't hurt him. Just keep him still a while longer. I think I can see something...'

Identifying the trouble, Gina was able to remove the culprit grass seed and clean the ear as Basil lay motionless. 'That should do the trick.' She sighed in satisfaction, resting back on her haunches. Depositing the offending seed on a piece of lint, she showed it to the boy.

'Just that? But it's so small.' He frowned, unimpressed.

She nodded. 'Small but very vexing. I'm going to give you some ear drops too, just to clear some of the wax at the bottom of the canal. If he has any more trouble, you must bring him in to see me straight away.'

Damian nodded enthusiastically.

'He's been an exceptional patient,' she praised. 'A less obedient dog might well have had to be anaesthetised. He's very well-trained. Did you go to obedience classes?'

Damian flushed with pride. 'My dad took me. Basil was the best there and after six months we got a blue card and a certificate.'

Basil sprang to his feet, wagging his black tail ferociously, offering his paw and, as she laughingly took it, she told Damian to go along to Bev who would give him the prescription and, as a special reward, some doggie treats for Basil.

Boy and dog disappeared, passing Ben on the way as he strode into her room. 'You've a visitor,' he told her. 'I think you'd better leave the last few to me.'

She frowned, the smile drifting from her lips, her violet eyes puzzled. 'I wouldn't dream of it–'

Tilting his dark head in the direction of the car park, he interrupted her sharply, 'You'd better hurry; he's waiting for you outside. It's Kieron Brent.'

CHAPTER EIGHT

It was, Gina thought as she walked out of the surgery, like being halfway into reading a book, then flipping the pages backwards instead of forwards.

For months after the accident, she had dreamed of being able to walk, unaided, towards Kieron Brent. And here she was, doing just that, asking herself in amazement as she drew nearer what she had ever seen in him.

Five years older than she, he remained a very good-looking man with wavy blond hair swept away from an intelligent forehead and charming blue eyes. But, in spite of the image, the sleek car on which he leaned in that casual pose, everything she had ever felt for him paled into insignificance compared to what she felt...

It was then that her sure steps halted as the truth hit her. Ben Cassell occupied every corner of her mind, no matter how intense her struggle had been not to let him into her heart.

Realising Kieron was staring curiously at her, she held out her hand, the sudden understanding of how she felt about Ben making her fingers tremble slightly before she was able to compose herself.

'Gina!' Kieron ignored the hand and would have embraced her had she not instinctively drawn back.

She could hardly believe he was here, larger than life, after two years. Questions raced through her mind as she stared at him. Why had he suddenly turned up after all this time? And how had he found out where she was working? Restraining her curiosity, she asked, over-brightly and somewhat irrelevantly, 'A new car?'

He stroked the shiny bodywork. 'Do you like it?'

'It suits you.' Gina smiled, realising it was probably the replacement for the sports coupé in which they had crashed. But even the accident seemed distant now ... a part of her life that was in the past, the present so overwhelmingly intense.

'It's good to see you, Gina!' Kieron whistled through his teeth, observing instantly her slender figure under the white coat and her long ebony hair framing an oval face monopolised by huge violet eyes.

She smiled, remembering the familiar, easy way he had of charming. 'You haven't changed a bit!'

He grinned. 'Then you're pleased to see me?'

'I'm surprised!' She laughed lightly. 'Extremely.'

'Gina...' He moved towards her, glancing over her shoulder towards the practice. 'Is there somewhere we could talk, somewhere a little more private?'

She stiffened, suddenly aware of the intensity of the blue eyes and the vague sense of annoyance creeping over her that he could just descend like this and expect her to drop everything after two years. 'I'm sorry, Kieron, but we are extremely busy. The surgery is quite full–'

'Yes ... yes, forgive me; of course, I understand. It's just that–' he hesitated, looking uncomfortable '–it's been so long since we've seen one another. Listen, I'm staying the weekend with friends in Lilliput.' He reached out for her hands. 'Have dinner with me tomorrow evening?'

It was a shock to feel him touch her and she tried to withdraw her fingers. 'It's ... rather short notice ... and, as I told you, we are busy...'

'Please ... for old time's sake?' he persisted, not letting her go. 'Surely you can make time just for a meal? I promise to return Cinderella before midnight!' He laughed and, releasing her hands, leant back on the car, studying her.

She hesitated. 'I'm really not sure what I'll be doing...'

'Gina! Come on! What's the harm in dinner and a little friendly conversation? Surely you can make room in your busy schedule for just one evening's relaxation?'

She sighed. 'No, you haven't changed, Kieron!'

They both laughed and she found herself agreeing to see him the following evening, though, as she walked back to the surgery after seeing him off, she wondered whatever had possessed her. Some consolation was that over dinner she would no doubt discover exactly how he had found out about her and why he had decided to turn up after so long!

Giving a deep sigh as she walked into Reception, she was surprised to be met by Ben's grey eyes watching her. Moving across the room and taking her arm, he guided her into the hall and finally into her room.

'Ben ... whatever is the matter?' she asked as he deliberately shut the door behind them.

'Brent, as a matter of fact.' He thrust his hands deeply into the pockets of his white coat, obviously annoyed. 'You're heading for trouble ... much more trouble than you can handle. I know you're going to say it's none of my business, but if I can take advice from you on the subject of my daughter, then I think you can do the same as regards Brent. He's bad news for you, Gina, and as long as you work for me I can't just stand by and watch him wreck your life again.'

'Thank you,' she gasped, shocked, 'for your concern as my employer!' Her heart began to pound with the familiar rhythm that accompanied their arguments lately and this, it seemed, was the beginning of yet another. But whatever he had read into her meeting with Kieron was quite wrong and it certainly didn't give him the right to preach at her, employer or not!

'Don't you realise he's only using you?' Ben demanded, unwilling to let the subject drop, his large feet planted squarely on the floor.

'I'm not Kieron's puppet if that's what you mean and I certainly don't intend to be, and from now on I would prefer it if you–'

Both of them started as the door suddenly flew open. A man balancing a parrot cage in his arms almost fell in. 'I'm sorry to jump the queue,' he apologised breathlessly, with Vicki tugging at his arm, 'but I tried clipping my parrot's toenails and I've made one bleed and he's very upset. I … I'm really afraid he's losing a lot of blood.'

Gina took a deep breath and tried to form her face into placid serenity, silently remonstrating with herself for arguing with Ben. 'It's all right, Vicki,' she told the harassed nurse. 'I'll deal with it.'

After Vicki disappeared back to Reception she cast her eyes back to her employer. 'If there's nothing more?' she asked frostily.

171

Nodding curtly, he left the room and she gave a long inner sigh. Boss or no boss, he had no right to challenge her personal life, even if for a few minutes it had encroached on her professional time.

'I got an awful fright,' the man was saying nervously as she gestured him in, trying to concentrate. 'The man at the pet-store told me how to do it when I bought Roberto. That was a couple of years ago ... perhaps I'd forgotten what he told me and did something wrong?'

He removed the cloth from the cage. Roberto was not on a perch but huddled, fluffed up, in a corner.

'He's a Yellow-Fronted Amazon, isn't he?' Gina asked, feeling instant sympathy for the caged bird.

'That's right. Not brought over in a squashed cage with hundreds of others, though. He's hand-reared in England.'

But he's in a small cage now, Gina thought regretfully. 'Have you brought Roberto in to see us before?'

'No. He's normally very healthy. It's just his toenails are so long.' The parrot, with his lovely yellow crown and orange eyes, shuffled against his seed-tray.

'I'm going to have to take a look, so I'll need you to hold him steady. I think you may need these.' She handed the owner a pair of leather gloves. 'Hold his head between thumb and index finger, restraining his wings with the rest of your hand. For nail-clipping or bill-trimming this is the best way, unless, of course, your pet is very tame.'

Without too much chaos, Roberto restrained and safe in the man's grasp, Gina offered the bird a perch from the cage to clutch.

'The wound's coagulated already,' she explained as she examined him. 'You've actually cut the quick, not the vessel, which is lucky. The blood vessels extend two-thirds down into the nails and you have to be very careful.' Using styptic cotton and liquid anticoagulant to deal with the injury, she slowly corrected the shape of his claws with clippers.

Roberto wriggled himself free as he was returned to his cage. 'I'd recommend a much larger cage or an aviary,' Gina advised firmly, 'and lots of wood to chew.' As if in agreement, Roberto spread his wings, exhibiting the dazzling red streaking and yellowish-green of his exotic plumage, uttering an ear-piercing screech.

Gina watched them go, reflecting how much birds in captivity saddened her. Not unlike her own situation lately, where she was beginning to feel imprisoned by these emotions that had overwhelmed her for Ben. His reaction to Kieron had made her angry – had he really imagined she would be

173

so foolish as to pick up the threads with Kieron again? Perhaps he thought that, if she was going to be involved in a re-kindling of a relationship, her professional work would suffer?

Her eyes smarted suddenly. Heavens! She wasn't going to break down here ... not at work!

Blowing her nose, she made a supreme effort. By the time Vicki brought in the next client she was reasonably composed. The wire-haired terrier Tojo had been brought in to her last week with an abscess. He looked very affronted to have the encumbrance of the Elizabethan collar, the only remedy for the nasty infection under his tail.

Once he was on the treatment table she examined him. 'The antibiotic and the collar seem to have worked. The infection has cleared up nicely,' she was pleased to say.

'Does he have to keep the collar on any longer?' his lady owner asked. 'He's a different dog with it. I used to think I would do anything to keep him out of mischief but I really miss the old Tojo. He doesn't even want his walk.'

Gina nodded and unclipped the collar. 'Be a good boy and leave your tail alone,' she warned Tojo. 'If he starts to worry it again, he'll undo all the good, so you'll have to watch him very closely, and at night-times; if he resorts to self-mutilation you will have to put it back on him,' she told his owner.

The terrier stretched, creased his body around to sniff his tail and, at the instant protest of both his owner and Gina, decided not to investigate further.

The afternoon kept her busy enough, but it was with difficulty that she kept her mind on her work. Just as she was trying to decide if there were some eggs remaining in the fridge for an omelette she heard Ben's familiar footfall in the corridor and was surprised to see him step into her room.

'All finished?' he asked pleasantly enough.

She nodded, aware of her inner reaction again at the sight of him, a tremor on her lips and a sudden influx of warm blood in her face, her feelings towards him so complex that it was a few seconds before she answered. 'Y-yes. I was just going actually... I've hardly spoken to Stuart. Has he left?'

'He had to shoot off to the dentist. Listen, do you feel like a reviver? I thought about The Plough, the little pub on the main road?'

She frowned. 'I don't think that's very wise at the moment, do you?'

'Coward!' he softly mocked, drawing a reciprocal smile from her lips. 'Truce? And anyway I'm on call, so I don't promise you we'll have time for more than a quick drink.'

Not wanting the gap to widen between them, she nodded hesitantly. 'All right, but give me a few moments to freshen up. I feel a wreck.'

His smile lingered while he stood there, watching her as she gathered her things. 'Take your time,' he said slowly and, with his gaze running over her dark hair, her slender, reed-like body as she took off her white coat, added pensively, 'You'll never even get near to looking like a wreck ... quite the opposite. You're...' And, as she turned, surprised by the huskiness in his voice, he finished, 'One of the most beautiful women I've ever seen, as a matter of fact.'

Gina let the air leave her lungs on a shocked sigh as she ducked past him and headed for the cloakroom. Did he really believe she was beautiful? Sarah had been so stunning, so lovely – in her shadow, she felt anything but the most beautiful woman he had ever seen! She was everything that Sarah was not. Dark where Sarah was fair, oval face rather than heart-shaped, taller whereas Sarah had looked so dainty and petite. Her fingers quivered as she tried to apply a light coat of lipstick and finally gave up, the effort far too risky, as it was only then that she realised just how badly she was shaking.

The Plough was almost deserted save for another couple propping up the bar. Ben ordered shandy for himself and a small pale sherry for Gina since she was not driving.

'Good?' Ben asked as they sat in the most comfortable corner on well-worn crimson velour seats.

'Delicious,' she murmured, reflecting that the last time they had sat like this was at the Lovers Crossed. It seemed like an eternity ago now.

'About this afternoon...' he began broodingly and Gina stiffened as he frowned at her. 'I was clumsy ... I don't seem to be able to strike quite the right note, do I?'

'It depends,' she answered carefully, thankful that now her body seemed to be back in control, probably aided by the warming quality of the sherry. 'I prefer we talk about the present, Ben, and not the past.'

'I agree.' He grinned, meeting her eyes. 'You can't ever re-create the past. It took me quite a while to learn that. But it's true, you know. Like going back to childhood ... visiting somewhere you grew up ... it's never the same when you return. Always a little disappointing.'

Point taken, she thought, smiling a little, but what Ben didn't seem to understand was that she had no interest in Kieron and she was bitterly regretting having agreed to seeing him again. Not only was it a waste of a good evening, but there was no logic in accepting the invitation other than at the time it enabled her to wriggle out of a rather disagreeable conversation.

She was on the point of changing the subject when the faint purr of the bleeper echoed from Ben's breast-pocket.

Grinning at him, she laughed lightly and said, 'Saved by the bell.'

He nodded, white teeth glimmering as he laughed too. 'I said I didn't think we would have very long to talk, but this is ridiculous!'

'Maybe it's just as well,' she murmured ruefully, beginning to stand up.

He laid a large hand on hers, causing the reaction she was becoming to accept as normal, warm blood turning her cheeks a whirlpool of dusky pink. 'Stay where you are and finish your sherry,' he suggested calmly. 'Though I have to say you don't seem to need much colour added to that lovely complexion.'

Flushing even deeper, Gina sat down again and picked up her small glass. She watched his large, retreating figure as he walked out of The Plough, going to the Discovery to take the call.

She pushed her own drink away with a deep sigh.

Wishing irritably once again that she had not allowed herself to be persuaded into going out with Kieron, she tried to think of a way out of the date. Why, oh, why hadn't she thought to take the phone number of his friends?

Ben was scribbling on a pad as she walked over to the vehicle parked under the pub's bright lights. With her coat unnecessarily wrapped firmly around her, she felt the warmth of spring evening air on her cheeks and reflected how unusually mild and sunny the weather was just now, for the time of year. Summer, it seemed, was only a breath away.

'A Shetland, of all things,' Ben muttered, engrossed in his thoughts as he wrote. 'About a mile from here. Found on the road. Obviously escaped. They've taken it in to the police-house garden.'

'Is it hurt?'

'The wife of the local policeman isn't sure. She can see some bleeding on its back, but she doesn't know anything about ponies and won't go too near. Her twelve-year-old son managed to coax it into the garden, so Vicki says.'

'I'll come with you.'

He looked up at her. 'I don't think there's any call for you to come. I'll drop you home first.'

'But isn't the police station just north of here? We're close to it, aren't we?'

He tucked the pad into the dashboard clip. 'No sense in dragging you out.'

'You'll need someone to steady the pony if you treat it.'

He thought for a moment then shrugged.

'All right. If you like.'

They drove to the police house not far along the road, a rural detached red-brick house next door to the equally small police station. As they arrived two policemen, one who seemed to have a definite limp, climbed into a police car and drove off. Ben nodded towards the house. 'I came out here once to treat a collie, about three years ago.'

The woman was waiting at the side-gate, a young child astride her hip and a boy standing beside her who pulled open the gate.

'Mr Cassell? I remember you came last time.' She smiled at Gina, handing over a head collar. 'You might need this. The pony's frisky.'

'Mrs Berry, isn't it?' Ben grinned and ruffled the boy's hair. 'Nice to see you again. How is your dog?'

'Died last year, I'm afraid. He was twelve and he had a long life, thanks to you. My husband says that op you did gave him another three years.'

'I had to do a surgical repair of a tendon,' Ben explained to Gina.

'He went peacefully in his sleep,' Mrs Berry added. 'And, because of his op, he was as fit as some dogs I've seen of five and six.'

Mrs Berry led the way around into half an acre of fenced grass and fruit trees. At the far end a small brown Shetland eyed them

180

shiftily below a thick fringe of dark hair.

'Robin caught him, though it's a miracle he did,' Mrs Berry grinned. 'I warn you, my husband, who you've just seen driving off, tried to put a head collar on him and the little devil trod on his foot.'

'You've no idea where he came from, I suppose?' Gina asked, smiling sympathetically.

'No ... but his owner's bound to ring the station saying they've lost a lively little chap like him. He's someone's pride and joy, that's for sure.' She sighed as she turned away. 'Now you'll have to excuse me because I'm just going to put Emma to bed. Call me if you want me, mind.'

Ben grinned at Gina when they were on their own. 'Any suggestions?'

She laughed lightly. 'There are two of us! And we do have a head collar.'

'To a truculent Shetland that's probably a joke!'

They began to walk slowly along the path when the pony shook its mane and snorted, taking off from beneath the apple tree with the speed of lightning.

'Watch out!' Ben yelled and, clasping her firmly by the waist, swept her out of the way in the nick of time. 'Are you OK?' he asked, concerned, as she stood dazed.

'Y–yes ... I think so; I wasn't ready for that.'

He grinned down at her. 'I won't dwell on it, but the last thing you want at the moment is to be knocked off your feet by a charging pony.'

She nodded with a sigh, catching her breath.

He seemed reluctant to let her go as he steadied her with his large hands and, with a long finger trailed a strand of hair from her eyes. 'Come on, let's try this from another angle, a safer one.'

As they reached the gate the Shetland, apparently remorseful for its behaviour, trotted up behind, watching them as they left the field.

Ben laughed aloud. 'Did I say Shetlands have a mind of their own? I have a feeling it isn't an adequate description!' His hand was still lightly supportive around her waist as they stared at the pony over the fence.

'He's quick, isn't he?' said a small voice beside them.

'Robin ... hello!' Ben smiled at the boy who climbed on to the bottom strut of the fence, watching the pony with interest. 'Yes, very quick,' Ben agreed. 'Obviously he's not hurt at all ... except for that gash on his side. It's quite deep by the looks of it.'

'Will you have to stitch him up?'

Ben nodded. 'Afraid so. Persuading him to stand still while I do it is another matter!'

'If you gave him sugar,' Robin suggested

brightly, 'he'd probably stay still.'

Gina glanced at Ben. 'Is that how you managed to get him in here?'

The boy nodded. 'I wanted to put the head collar on him, but Dad said he'd do it … only he didn't give him any sugar either.'

They all laughed as she whispered in Ben's ear, 'Why didn't we think of the obvious?'

Robin grinned. 'I could put the head collar on him … if you want.'

'He's all yours.' Ben handed over the head collar and they watched the boy disappear into the house. A few seconds later he emerged with his pockets full. Mrs Berry looked out from the kitchen window as the powerful security light illuminated the garden.

The Shetland trotted over without hesitation. Soon he was crunching on the tit-bit, oblivious of all else except what was coming from Robin's pockets.

Ben raised his eyebrows, grinning wryly. As they moved in closely he warned, 'The worst part will be putting in local anaesthetic and the injections to numb the area.'

'Perhaps if I hold the head collar?' Gina suggested, carefully avoiding the muddy brown hooves which had danced like a ballerina down the field. 'And then Robin can concentrate on feeding him the sugar.'

'Sugar's not really so good for them, is it?' Robin frowned.

'In this case, he could have caviare if it kept him quiet,' Ben laughed, laying his case down by the fence.

Surprisingly the little pony shuffled and bobbed as the anaesthetic went into the wound, but he seemed to be happy enough to crunch slowly on the knobs of sugar from Robin's pocket.

'It seems like five hours, not five minutes, waiting for it to take effect.' Gina sighed, smiling ruefully over the thick mat of brown horse hair and she caught Ben's reciprocatory smile. The light caught his smiling grey eyes and the coppery hair with deep golden lights lying untidily around his face.

'I'm going to fill the syringe and give him an injection, Robin.' Ben paused thoughtfully. 'Be careful he doesn't buck!' But Ben had hardly issued the warning, sliding the needle in, when the pony jerked back his head, almost knocking the syringe out of his hand. He trotted in a full circle around the garden before stopping with a cantankerous look in his deep brown eyes.

With great presence of mind, Robin darted across to the gate where he had hidden a reserve supply of carrots with fresh green tops. Soon order was restored as the temptation was too much to resist.

'One more injection,' Ben called, 'then we can leave him for ten minutes and let him have his head for a while before we put the stitches in.'

The second injection passed without event and, as they watched from the gate, the pony nuzzled the grass with his teeth, looking up occasionally to see if there was anything more tempting on offer.

Eventually, Ben gave Robin the signal and, with a quick squirt of antibiotic, put in six neat sutures followed by the anti-tetanus. With the delicate operation over, waiting docilely by the gate as they collected their things together, the pony followed their departure with a whinny of triumph. Gina stroked his tousled mane over the fence and gave him one last sugar-cube she had been saving for an emergency.

'He'll need those stitches out in a week,' Ben told Mrs Berry. 'So the owner must be told when he comes. And the next question is, how escape-proof is your garden? Can you keep him there until the owner is found?'

'Tom said the pony can stay ... there's nothing in the garden to spoil; it's all grass and weeds and trees. He's welcome to eat that if he wants. And Robin will check the fencing. He loves horses, helps out at the stables at weekends as a stable boy – but he wants to be a jockey eventually,' she added proudly.

After their goodbyes, Ben started up the Discovery and flicked on the headlights.

From the garden a familiar snorting erupted. Gina glanced at Ben and they both laughed. 'I'll come equipped with a pocket full of sugar-knobs when I take those stitches out in a week's time.' Ben grinned. 'Quite a formidable little character, wasn't he? Perhaps I'll be able to persuade Robin to help me again.'

'Robin's small for his age, isn't he?' Gina murmured, thinking about the remark his mother made about his becoming a jockey. 'He's only three years younger than Harriet and yet he's half her size.'

Ben frowned and nodded slowly. 'I hadn't thought, but yes, I suppose he is. He seems like a kid, whereas Harry is...'

'Already a young woman,' Gina finished softly for him.

There was a pause before Ben replied. 'You know, suddenly I realise she is, but I just can't see how it's happened.'

'Girls mature quicker than boys ... one day they are just little girls, the next, fully grown women. It's just as confusing for them. My father never really managed to accept the fact until I left for college.'

Ben glanced at her quickly. 'You're drawing a parallel. Do you think I'm refusing to accept Harriet's maturity?'

She hesitated, remembering how she had not appreciated Ben's comments on Kieron, however well-meant.

Ben caught the indecision and added quietly, as he cast his eyes back to the road. 'You needn't answer. I've a pretty good idea anyway.'

He said it without rancour and Gina didn't press to make conversation. It wasn't necessary, it seemed, with Ben absorbed in his own thoughts and she in hers. Perhaps if she managed to ride this unhappy impasse they'd developed between them regarding their personal affairs she would be able to forget or even conquer the powerful feelings she had allowed to swamp her. Then, and only then, would she be able to get on with her life objectively.

'Here we are...' Ben said suddenly. And she saw that they were already home. The lights blazed from the cottage and a dark blue saloon car was parked in the car park.

'You've a visitor,' Gina said, recognising it at once.

Ben frowned. 'Oh, – yes ... Viv. It'll be something to do with Harvey, no doubt,' he said with a sigh.

'I'm going to check with Vicki on the enteritis case and the spayings,' she muttered as she climbed out.

'I hardly think that's necessary.' He stood in front of her as they met head-on by the nose of the Discovery. 'The nurses can cope very well with the recovery-room patients; you should know that by now.'

'If you've no objection, I would still like to check for myself,' she answered perversely, knowing full well that she wouldn't have a chance of settling down until she had worked herself into tiredness this evening.

She saw his face harden. The wide shoulders shrugged as he said curtly, 'Please yourself, if you want to end up with exhaustion.' Then he strode off without a word more.

Seeing him walk to the cottage as she herself went to the practice, she felt a deep, gnawing ache inside, a pain which seemed to grow out of all proportion as she watched him disappear into the cottage and almost certainly into the arms of Vivienne Armitage.

She glanced up to see Harriet's light on in her bedroom. Feeling instant sympathy for the girl, she reminded herself that Ben's business was his own. He himself had proved that particular point today!

Later, after checking the recovery-room patients and finding them, as Ben had foretold, perfectly well, she walked back to the annexe. Vivienne's car was still parked where it had been on their arrival. Harriet's light still blazed from upstairs and the drawing-room curtains were closed, a chink of light signalling a cosy light behind.

Just before bed, Gina found herself peering out of the bay window for the car ... and, discovering it gone, tried to reconcile the feeling of overwhelming relief at its disappearance with her new resolution not to get mixed up in Ben's life. Hopefully, if she drew on all her resources, she would not then be destined for unhappiness, the inevitable unhappiness akin to no other – that of unrequited love.

CHAPTER NINE

Gina realised she was developing a headache.

Had Kieron always been so self-absorbed? Did his blue eyes always flash too dramatically along with the practised smile of white teeth? Or had she simply never noticed before?

In the expensive restaurant, after their meal, looking at him across the table, seeing the handsome, unworried expression, she was shocked at the super-imposed ghost of another face in her mind, her imagination bringing to life a man with thick coppery hair and perceptive grey eyes.

'Do you know, Gina,' Kieron was saying, leaning across the table, 'this has been a wonderful evening? Just like old times. I've thought of you so often and wondered how you were.'

'You have?' Gina frowned, aware of Kieron's fingers creeping slowly along her wrist.

He paused, smiling. 'I heard about your recovery from the local grapevine. You know how it is with our profession. I always knew you had it in you to prove those doctors wrong.'

Gina felt the blood drain from her face. How did he have the nerve to say that? Was she really hearing this from the man who had deserted her while she was in hospital, the man who had assumed her career was over as she lay helplessly in bed?

His fingers tightened around her arm. 'When Dudley retires next month, he's moving, lock, stock and barrel. The flat is large and comfortable over the practice ... well, I don't have to tell you – you know, you've seen it–'

'I don't think I understand you, Kieron,' she interrupted, hardly able to believe her ears.

'I'm offering you ... asking you ... if you'll come back to the practice. You always said your dream was to live above the shop – I could make that dream come true.'

'You ... you want me to move in with you?'

He sighed. 'Don't make it sound as if I'm propositioning you! We talked about marriage often enough, didn't we? If only that damn accident hadn't happened, by now we would probably have been settled, with a home of our own. I knew it was a terrible mistake when we parted.'

She shook her head, her lips quivering. 'Kieron, we parted because you discovered you might have an invalid on your hands, a wife who wouldn't be able to pull her weight in either a domestic or a professional sense! That was the real reason for the end of our relationship; there was no other.'

He stiffened, the smile fading from his lips, blue eyes cooling. 'Don't be absurd, Gina! How could you think such a thing?'

'Oh, quite easily. I've had two years to think about it very carefully.' It was no use, she thought, wishing she had never agreed to come tonight. 'I'm sorry, but it's too late to try to pick up where we left off. I don't want to marry you, Kieron, and, to be blunt, I think we would have made a disastrous mistake if we had married.'

'There's someone else!' he gasped. 'You wouldn't refuse me otherwise.'

'No, no one else.' Withdrawing her hands, she clutched her bag as the picture of deep grey eyes and a slow, serious smile filled her mind, mocking her denial. 'I like my job here, Kieron. I wouldn't give it up.'

'But it's only a locum's job! How long will you stay – six months, twelve?' he protested. 'There's no future in it. By marrying me you would have security and a career ahead of you.'

'My job has nothing to do with why I'm refusing you,' she answered firmly.

'Then it's Ben Cassell, isn't it?' Kieron muttered. 'I suppose I knew it was likely when I first talked to him.'

'You barely spoke to him!' She gasped in horror. 'You really shouldn't jump to such ridiculous conclusions!'

'There was something in his eyes...' Kieron accused, his voice hard. 'Something I didn't like. And I was quite sure he didn't want me to speak to you.'

'Heavens above!' She stared at him incredulously. 'You were imagining things!'

He laughed bitterly. 'You always were naïve, Gina. You don't seem to have improved any.'

'If I was naïve Kieron,' she bit back, deeply hurt, 'it was only because I was too frightened to accept the truth ... that we weren't right for one another.'

He shrugged. 'I admit that might have been true then, but when I saw you yesterday and you looked so well, even better than I'd heard–'

'So your visit was planned?' She gave a wry little smile. 'And you found me well enough to consider a proposal appropriate?' She felt a sharp pang of pity, grateful for seeing clearly now the enormity of the mistake she had been saved from making. She stood up, suddenly very weary and longing to be home. 'I think I'd like to go now, Kieron. It's been a lovely evening, but I am very tired.'

'Let's talk about this, Gina.' He shrugged, giving a charming smile. 'We'll have a drink in the bar?'

'No ... I'm quite exhausted after this week... I'm not used to late nights any more.' And, with that, she moved out of the restaurant, waiting for Kieron in the cool evening air. When he appeared by her side, his cheeks were flushed.

'No late nights? How remarkable, since your boyfriend only lives next door.'

She looked at him with clear contempt. 'Despite what you may think, Ben isn't my lover.'

'Then why can't we...?' He stopped, frowning heavily.

'Kieron, let's end the evening on a friendly note. We've known each other too long to quarrel like this.'

Somehow, she managed to keep the flow of conversation going. It wasn't easy and her nerves were tense as he occasionally stretched out his hand and touched her knee or arm while he drove.

The annexe appeared in the headlights and she gave an inner sigh of relief as he pulled on the hand-brake.

'Thank you for a pleasant evening,' she said as he insisted on walking her to her door.

When they arrived, he caught her by the arm. 'Ask me in for a nightcap, Gina?'

As though anticipating her refusal, he pulled her into his arms. His lips were hot and insistent as he kissed her, his hands travelling over her back as she tried to break free.

A dazzling light focused on them suddenly and Kieron let go, blinking, shielding his eyes with his hand. 'Who the hell is that?'

She didn't know and didn't care. The distraction gave her the perfect opportunity to twist her key in the lock and hurry in. It was a coward's way, she thought as she called out goodnight, but it was certainly effective.

There were voices outside as she slid the bolt across the top of the door and drew the safety-chain. One of them was Kieron's, but her heart was beating too frantically to catch the other and soon they drifted away, leaving her in silence. She walked into the flat slowly and switched on the lights, sinking into a chair with a long sigh. She wouldn't ever like to have to undergo an evening like that again!

Kieron would find someone else. Admirers were always plentiful around him, with those sort of looks, the 'little boy lost' expression which hid the ambitious, career-minded man beneath. Though it was hardly a compliment, he had offered her marriage when it was quite obvious that he regarded her primarily as an investment for the future now that she was able to practice again. At thirty-one he was looking for a partner in a business arrangement which happened to involve marriage as a side-clause!

Perhaps it was then, in the quietness, that she finally accepted the fact that, whether she liked it or not, Kieron had correctly sensed her feelings for Ben. He had misinterpreted Ben's, of course. The expression he had registered in his eyes had been merely territorial. An employer facing a threat to the equilibrium of his staff.

But as for her?

After tonight ... there was no point in trying to deceive herself any longer. She was deeply in love with Ben, recklessly in love, loving a man who could never love back. Not love her, at least, the way she needed to be loved. He was attracted physically ... but that wasn't love. Hadn't he told her on the day of her interview that he had no interest in marrying again?

Vivienne was the type of woman who would compromise. She would accept what Ben cared to offer in love's place ... but then, Vivienne was welcome!

Mrs Swain's cheerful, 'Halloo!' roused her as she walked past the cottage on Monday.

Harriet rushed out, hauling a crammed school-bag over her shoulder. 'Gina! We've just had a letter from Nana! She's coming to stay ... you'll be able to meet her! I've told her all about you over the telephone!'

Gina smiled in spite of her aching head

and weary body.

The trauma of the weekend over, she had to pull herself together, to find a way through the emotional upheaval which threatened both her chances of succeeding at this job and her own self-esteem which she had so long fought to recover through her illness.

Managing a bright smile, she said cheerfully, 'That's great for you, Harriet ... how are the kittens?'

'Marvellous! Guess what? I'm coming in to help out at the practice, over the Easter hols. You know, cleaning out the cages and walking the boarders, that sort of thing.'

So ... Ben had talked with his daughter? She stood listening to Harriet, her own words resurrected in her mind of the evening she had spent under Ben's roof. 'Talk to her, Ben!' she had advised, and obviously – and successfully – he had done just that. More than she could say for herself. It seemed that Ben was rapidly taking stock of his life, while she...

'I'm getting some extra pocket money,' Harriet was saying and Gina nodded, witnessing an astonishing change in Harriet, in her eyes especially, so bright and unguarded this morning.

'And that's the other thing!' Harriet added excitedly as though she had just remembered. 'Daddy says he's going to ask you if you'll come with us. Oh, you will come, won't you? If you don't like the cinema, we can go to the theatre. Please say you will?'

'I ... I can't impose, Harriet!' Gina felt her blood running cold. From now on, she must make every effort to keep distanced, to save what little pride she had and to shield herself from any more heartache.

'Why?' Harriet stood motionless, her face bewildered. 'Don't you want to come with us? Would you be bored?'

'No, of course not!'

'It's that man who came to see you on Friday, isn't it?' Harriet looked petulant, her eyes narrowing. 'I suppose he's your boyfriend and he wouldn't want you spending your time with us.'

'You mean Kieron?' Gina asked, frowning deeply.

'Mrs Swain saw him talking to you on Friday and asked me if I knew who it was. I asked Daddy and he got annoyed with me and told me it wasn't any of my business. So I supposed it was an old boyfriend or something.'

Gina shook her head. 'Kieron is just someone I knew from Surrey, that's all.'

'He certainly didn't seem like a "someone", the way he was trying to kiss you on Saturday night!'

'You saw...?' Gina gasped.

Harriet nodded, flushing at her outburst. 'Oh ... I'm sorry, Gina, I shouldn't have said that. But you see, Daddy had just come home from an emergency house-call and his headlights picked you out. I was looking from my bedroom window.'

Gina sighed and gave a small shrug. 'It's not what you think, Harriet ... but I can't explain now ... your bus is due, isn't it?'

'You're not angry with me ... are you?' Harriet looked so miserable, Gina smiled and shook her head.

'Of course I'm not. But you'd better hurry...'

The girl ran for her bus down the lane and Gina walked into surgery, her legs feeling like lead. It shouldn't matter that Ben would now think that she and Kieron were involved but, somehow, it did.

Saying good morning to the girls and Stuart, she hurried into her room, avoiding Ben's. Her first patient, an elderly Labrador bitch, presented a firm, hard swelling of the mammary gland along with weight loss, lethargy and weakness. Gina's heart sank as she looked at the worried couple, their eyes betraying their fear.

'I shall have to take a biopsy,' she explained gently to the Johnsons, 'and then we'll have to wait for the pathology report to come back.'

'How long will that be?' they asked.

'About a week, if you can bring her back tomorrow for the biopsy.'

Afterwards, Gina turned to the window and gazed out. Suddenly the view was a complete blur. Quite illogically, tears sprang to the corners of her eyes and she pulled out a tissue, wiping them away impatiently.

Turning around, she found Ben studying her, his expression darkening as he looked into her eyes. Before she could move, his arms slid around her, pressing her face into the hard wall of his chest. 'Hey ... what's this?' she heard him murmur above her. 'You're upset?'

Furiously she shook her head, trying to push away from him, but he held her firm, running his large hand over her hair.

Eventually she levered herself apart from him, looking up into his concerned grey eyes. She stifled the sense of desolation at his tenderness, her heart fluttering wildly in her breast as she set her teeth firmly together behind compressed lips.

'Do you want to talk about what's worrying you?' he asked softly.

She shook her head. 'No, I'm fine now ... thanks. It was nothing. I'm probably over-reacting with my patients, that's all.'

Dark eyebrows arched questioningly. 'Is that the truth? I'm more inclined to think it's Brent who's on your mind!'

She couldn't speak, not without bursting into tears, and there was no way she was going to let that happen again.

'You're letting him hurt you all over again,' he said with sudden violence in his voice. 'Can't you see it?'

She couldn't deny his accusation. How could she confess that her tears were not for Kieron without giving away her true feelings? It was probably better, in view of the circumstances, to let him think what he liked.

He went still, regarding her in brooding silence, until the door swung open and Vicki gazed in at them both. 'Ben … there's a call for you … a farmer with a calving problem. And Gina, an emergency...' Behind her followed an older man carrying a small black and tan dog in his arms.

Gina did not see the going of Ben. With swift movements she gestured the man to lay his dog on her treatment table and snatched up her stethoscope.

When she found a heartbeat she nodded to Vicki who was already tearing the wrapper from a fresh syringe in order to give an injection of stimulant.

The man pulled a handkerchief out of his pocket and wiped his brow. 'What is it? What's wrong?'

'He's suffered a heart attack. How old is he?' Gina asked calmly.

'Eight … a bit more, perhaps. It happened so quickly! We were in the park just walking … and then … he sort of keeled over.'

Gina nodded. 'I'm going to give him a heart and respiratory injection, which may bring him around.'

During the next few minutes, there was a slight flicker of response from the closed eyelids. She found a stronger heartbeat and, looking with sympathy at the elderly pensioner, she suggested he sit beside his dog.

Whispered words of encouragement seemed to help as first the dachshund began to shake and shiver. Then the small round button of a nose twitched and life flowed slowly through the body.

As time wore on, all the dog's faculties returned and he even managed to lick his owner's hand. 'There seems no permanent damage done,' Gina explained. 'But, as always with a dog of this age, there's a possibility of a recurrence. You must keep to the medication I give you. It's very important.'

'A lucky recovery on the dachs this morning.' Vicki sighed as she followed Gina in to the staffroom at lunchtime.

'I just hope his heart holds out.' Gina frowned worriedly. 'To be honest, I was surprised when he came around so quickly and stabilised.'

'Love for his master,' Vicki suggested philosophically.

True enough, Gina reflected over her snatched lunch. Love turned a coward into a hero, a plain woman into a ravishing beauty. Love worked miracles, but even a miracle could not transform the love Ben still preserved in his heart for Sarah into love for another, living human being. And she had decided she wouldn't take second-best, decided that she would be no threat to the other woman in his life...

She saw more than her usual quota during the afternoon: booster vaccinations, injuries from scrapes and even a depressed tortoise, but the last on the afternoon's list, a perineal hernia on a terrier, had to be booked in for surgery the following week. Teatime found her in the office fighting with the next day's overbooked lists.

When she finally locked up, Ben had wandered in, hair falling untidily over his forehead and a lion's share of mud on his cheeks.

'Successful afternoon?' she enquired ruefully.

'Depends what you mean by successful.' He grinned at her, lifting a questioning eyebrow and then, catching her amusement, his face lit up with a smile that made her realise just what a devastatingly handsome face it was when brightened by laughter.

'The calf was coming out backwards as I arrived and got stuck at the shoulder.' He chuckled derisively at himself. 'Luckily I won and just managed to turn him in time! You know, I've a feeling it's going to be one of those weeks.'

Words which were certainly true, Gina reflected over the next few days. Reluctant to let Ben see the outward signs of her depression, she made a concerted effort to throw herself into work.

It was only in the evenings when she returned to her flat that the full force of her despondency hit her, not even the success of the little enteritis case cheering her up as the dog's thin frame fleshed out.

Somehow she managed to get through the busy week, opting to stand in over the weekend for Stuart who had to attend a wedding. Though the Saturday and Sunday were relatively quiet, she welcomed the opportunity of the work to keep her mind fully absorbed.

Tuesday arrived along with the pathology report on the Labrador. The bad news came as no real shock, but there seemed a faint irony in Vicki's earlier observations as she wished away the task of telling the Johnsons that their pet's tumour was inoperable. Easter week, too ... a cruel blow.

But, when the Labrador padded tiredly down the passageway to her room, she sensed that the couple had already prepared themselves. The bitch wearily slumped on the consulting-room floor, her white whiskers and bristle of chin resting on the outstretched paws, and the final, sad farewells were said.

Ben came into her consulting-room after

the Johnsons left. 'I know how you're feeling,' he consoled her. 'But think how much worse it must be for doctors who have to watch their patients suffer. Get your work into perspective and you'll feel a lot better.'

She nodded. 'I know. But what you were saying about this week ... it certainly seems to have been a testing time for me.'

'In more ways than one,' he remarked drily, a glitter in the perceptive grey eyes.

She paused. 'If you mean Kieron, Ben, no. I wasn't referring to him at all. I was just reflecting professionally – aloud – which–' she gave him a dubious smile '–I'm not sure I should do when you're around.'

He grinned. 'That's honest of you anyway .... but I'm harmless enough ... most of the time.'

'Full moon for instance?' She laughed lightly.

'How did you guess?'

'Witchcraft, of course, a gift from the cradle.' Her violet eyes laughed as they regarded him, the big man overshadowing her with the teasing, slightly crooked smile.

But his amusement died as slowly he nodded. 'You may be right there... I shouldn't be at all surprised if you cast spells...' His eyes held hers and she felt a warming flow of beautiful pleasure drive through her.

It was he who spoke first. 'I don't suppose

you've seen Harry, have you? She was going to walk a spaniel earlier, one that Stuart has in under observation.'

Gina swallowed on the lump in her throat, coming back to reality. 'Yes … yes… I think I saw her walking out with the Johnsons.'

More than pleased of the excuse to look for her, feeling the usual debilitating flush well on its way from neck to face, Gina headed into the corridor. A few moments later she and Ben discovered Harriet in the dispensary, blowing her nose.

'That old Labrador was such a lovely dog, wasn't she?' Harriet whispered shakily.

Ben glanced at Gina, sliding a comforting arm around his daughter's shoulders. 'Yes, she was, Harry. And she lived a long and happy life, we must all remember. Now the best thing would be for the Johnsons to look to the future and find themselves another companion.'

As usual, a flurry of activity outside disturbed the momentary peace. 'I'll go,' Gina said and, smiling at Harriet, she left father and daughter alone.

Preoccupied, she walked into her own room, almost to collide with a slim figure swathed in pastel blue.

'Vivienne!' she gasped.

The cool blonde smiled. 'Hello, Gina; we haven't seen much of one another, have we?'

Gina gazed at her uncertainly. 'No … but

206

if it's Ben you want–'

'All in good time,' Vivienne said sweetly and closed the door behind her. 'I wanted a quick word with you, actually. Ben tells me your parents live in the south?'

'Yes ... the Purbecks,' Gina answered uneasily.

'In which case you'll be going to see them during the Easter break, no doubt?'

'It depends on the rota, on who is on call.' Gina paused. 'I haven't made any special plans yet.'

'Oh!' Vivienne trailed a slim finger over the windowsill, staring out. 'A pity I didn't know before... I naturally assumed you had made arrangements. You see, Ben and I are giving a garden party up at the house for the staff and for our friends on Easter Monday. As a matter of fact, I'm hoping Audrey will be here in time.' Vivienne's smile was sweet but the light eyes were clear in their unfriendly message. 'Well, I mustn't keep you. Ben frowns on my distracting his staff. If you're free to come, do, by all means. Bring that nice young man of yours... I'd like to meet him.'

Gina caught her breath. 'Who are you talking about?'

Vivienne raised pert eyebrows. 'You didn't see me, did you, a couple of Saturdays ago? I was just leaving that cosy little restaurant on the harbour when you walked in with ...

what is your boyfriend's name?'

Gina paled. 'If you mean Kieron Brent, he isn't my boyfriend. He is the junior partner of the practice I worked for in Surrey just after I qualified–'

'Oh ... you needn't explain,' Vivienne interrupted smoothly. 'You made the perfect couple.'

Too shocked to speak, Gina saw the door open and Ben standing there, his frown deep as Vivienne swept across the floor, reached up and kissed him fully on the lips.

Gina felt nausea sweep through her as Vivienne's heels sank slowly back to the floor, her fingers lying on his arms.

Not wishing to overhear their conversation, Gina grappled for a veneer of cool efficiency to get her through the next few seconds as she bent her head to look blindly at the case-notes on her desk. The last thing she consciously registered was Ben's arm sliding around Vivienne's narrow waist, steering her out of the room and into the hall.

Her heart contracted as she thought of what she had just witnessed. Clearly identifying her feelings of rampant jealousy, she reached out a hand to steady herself on the chair.

'Gina ... are you all right?' Vicki asked as she came into the room to deliver fresh towels.

'Yes … yes,' Gina murmured. 'It's just so warm in here…'

But ordinary warmth wasn't the problem, Gina decided dismally as the nurse busied herself and finally left the room, it was the warmth of anger and jealousy. A potent combination heady enough to make life desperately unhappy, she was still thinking when, some time later, Ben reappeared. 'Road accident,' he said stiffly, supporting the limp shape of a fluffy white cat in his arms. 'I've a client in my room … may I come in?'

'Of course!' Gina sped over to help him, forgetting all else, laying her hands under the cat's head as they lowered him on her table.

'A faint heartbeat,' Ben told her seconds later, moving his stethoscope over the stained white fur. Then, shaking his head, he sighed. 'In coma … internal injuries … no wonder; it was a lorry, apparently, which hit him.'

A shudder passed through the body and, as Ben was about to fill a syringe, blood passed out from the mouth and trickled on to the table.

'No need,' Gina said with a sigh.

For a few seconds they both remained silent, then Ben looked up at her. 'Mercifully he never knew what happened, but the owner saw everything. She's very distressed.'

'I'll see her,' Gina offered, staring at his soiled white coat and hands. 'You'll need to wash and change – and your client is still waiting in your room.'

He nodded. 'Thanks ... but wait; I was going to have a word with Harry too. The woman was so desperate, she gave the cat to her instead of one of the nurses.'

'Oh, dear, poor Harriet. But don't worry; I'll find her.'

For a few seconds their eyes met, briefly, in perfect accord, and Gina yearned again to be close to him, to feel the pressure of those arms around her, to feel their strength and give in to the passion that burned inside her and yet would never have a chance of being set free.

The moment passing, she turned away and by sheer force of will hurried along the corridor. She eventually found both the owner and Harriet in the quiet room and they gazed up at her expectantly as she walked in, the woman's eyes red-rimmed with crying.

Gina shook her head. 'I'm so sorry ... we did all we could ... he didn't regain consciousness.'

The woman began crying softly and Harriet slid an arm around her shoulders. 'I'll make a cup of tea,' she told Gina. 'Don't worry. I'll stay with Mrs Hill for a while.'

'Are you sure?'

Harriet nodded and gave her a brave smile. Leaving them alone, Gina took a long deep breath, relieved that Harriet was taking the brunt so well. She seemed to be a natural with people and the incident with the cat had not appeared to upset her; in fact, she was handling the situation very maturely.

Which, she thought miserably, was more than she could say for herself, the picture of Vivienne Armitage standing on tiptoe to kiss Ben's mouth lying like a knife in between her ribs.

Gina saw to her next patient, then stood quietly, trying to reassemble her thoughts. She heard Ben's voice in the hall, deeply timbred and so familiar now.

He grinned as he drew level and saw her standing there. 'Rush over. Stuart still has two to see, but the open surgery is finished.' He frowned, tilting his head at her. 'How was Harry?'

'You needn't worry; she's fine.'

He gave a deep, relieved sigh, making his way in towards her. 'Thanks ... you were right about talking,' he said softly, gazing down at her, lifting a loose ebony skein of hair and tucking it behind her ear. 'We had a good heart to heart and it seems to have worked wonders.'

What was it she saw in those eyes which made her feel as if her bones were melting inside her skin?

It came to her quite clearly then, as she gazed into the face she loved so much, that she could no longer live her life in either Vivienne's shadow or Sarah's hallowed memory.

Her contract was up in May … and she would not renew it.

CHAPTER TEN

On the Wednesday of Easter week, Jake Forsythe phoned. Gina spoke to him in Ben's absence, relieved to hear that Chamois was slightly better, though Jake was cautious of laying the success with the sodium hyaluronate.

She made a memo of it and slipped it on to Ben's desk, only to be halted by yet another call as she reached her room. Kieron's voice came over with liquid ease.

'I'm sorry, Kieron, I can't talk; I'm really very busy!'

'Not too busy to come to a garden party with me on Easter Monday, though?' he persisted. 'A charming lady phoned me. I had no idea who she was at first, but she explained–'

Gina's fingers tightened on the receiver as she interrupted bluntly, 'I'm sorry, but I have other plans for Easter, Kieron,' and taking a deep breath and counting to ten, she managed to disentangle herself politely but firmly from the call, clamping down the phone with a groan.

The nerve of Vivienne Armitage! Was there no limit to her meddling? Luckily work drove

away her anger as a distressed pregnant spaniel whose labour had begun several hours ago
was hurried into her room. Her annoyance
quickly evaporating, she stroked the hot, silky
forehead of the dog with concern.

Two spinster sisters, Bella's owners, were
as nervous as Bella herself. 'We thought we
could manage the delivery,' tall Miss Ash
said, her thin face paling as Bella strained.

'It's been going on for ages,' small Miss
Ash added faintly.

Gina examined Bella, finding the cervix
open but with no sign of a puppy on its way.
'I will have to stimulate her contractions by
giving her an injection.'

She filled a syringe, gave the injection and
gently massaged the area. 'Try not to worry.
We'll see what results the injection brings;
meanwhile, would you both like a cup of
tea?'

It was all Gina could think of to lessen the
tension for Bella whose plaintive eyes were
fixed on her owners' distraught faces. As the
sisters drank their tea provided by Harriet
in the small, quiet room, alone Gina pondered on whether to perform a Caesarean.
She delayed, her instincts telling her that
perhaps, with a little breathing space, Bella
might produce naturally.

Ten minutes later Bella's straining finally
brought rewards. A glimpse of a miniature
liver-brown head prompted Gina to ease the

live puppy out gently and ask Vicki to return the Ash sisters in time for the second puppy's arrival.

'They're beautiful!' little Miss Ash gasped, putting a frail hand to her forehead and swaying.

'A chair, Vicki, please!' Gina called and the nurse swiftly propped a chair beneath Miss Ash's collapsing weight, just as Bella gave a satisfied shiver and began to lick her puppies.

The Ashes were speechless with delight over their new family ... and Gina felt a sudden pang of sympathy for them. Two spinsters, their world in Bella and her pups, never having had the experience of babies. Suddenly, she wondered if the same might not happen to her, falling in love with a man who could never return her love or her hopes for the future of sharing and creating a family out of that love. There would never be anyone else for whom she felt this way. Kieron had been a calf love, infatuation, but this was the real thing; she knew it now. The bleakness of her situation overwhelmed her. Ben had said he never envisaged marrying again. It seemed that he could never love another woman as he had loved Sarah. Which made Gina's position working here at the practice completely untenable, living next door to him, feeling the way she did.

The pang of anguish which gripped her heart was only eased by the resolution she had made to leave. The alternative – having an affair, rivalling Vivienne's position in his life – was unthinkable. Gina looked down at the picture of new life – Bella coiled with her offspring. A deep sigh rose up inside her and she forced herself to concentrate on the whimperings of joy which came from the new-born puppies and their mother.

'Can we take them home? Will they be all right now?' little Miss Ash asked.

Gina nodded. 'I'll give her an injection of antibiotic to offset any infection … just in case … then they must be left peacefully to feed and to sleep. Bella will need rest too, so be careful not to worry over her. If you're happy, she will be happy too.'

Happiness, recollected Gina as the Ashes departed, meant different things to different people. She had come to find happiness and heartache here, in this practice. But soon this building, her flat, the new life she had had such hopes for on her first day, would be part of her past.

The crunch of wheels over the gravel out-side caused her to glance through the open window. Ben pulled up in the Discovery, his large frame easily recognisable. Gina saw Harriet run from the surgery, her face full of excitement.

A few minutes later, Ben appeared at her door. 'Gina, have you a spare moment or two?' With a surprise she saw that he was dressed in a sleek dark suit, not his usual waxed jacket or sports coat. He looked so handsome, it took all her will-power to disguise her feelings and she nodded quickly, her heart lurching as she walked beside him.

Lyn Browning was on duty and Gina explained that she would be no more than a few moments, then, with Lyn's curious gaze following her, she went outside with Ben. The female passenger had alighted from the Discovery and walked towards them across the car park, Harriet beside her. As she came closer Gina found herself gazing into a pair of light blue eyes remarkably reminiscent of Harriet's.

'Gina, I'd like you to meet Audrey,' Ben said, his fingers slipping around her waist, pressing her forward.

Gina held out her hand, shocked at how sensitive her feelings were at meeting Sarah's mother. 'I'm very pleased to meet you, Mrs Farringdon.'

'Oh, please – Audrey!' smiled the small, youthful-looking woman with blonde-grey hair elegantly coiled up into a topknot, returning her handshake. 'I've heard so much about you, Gina.'

'From me.' Harriet grinned without embarrassment.

'And from Ben!' Audrey added calmly, casting a glance towards her son-in-law.

Gina tried to suppress her flush of embarrassment and was relieved when Harriet began to talk in her usual excited way, telling Gina about her grandmother's trip from Truro.

Eventually Audrey linked her arm through Harriet's. 'We mustn't keep you, Gina. I know you are busy in surgery... Ben explained ... but please come over and have some lunch with us ... presumably Ben does permit you a lunch-hour?' she asked ruefully.

Gina hesitated. 'You've been travelling since early this morning–'

'I've thoroughly enjoyed the comforts of British Rail, yes!' Audrey laughed dismissively. 'I love train journeys. Believe it or not they invigorate me. I feel very fresh – so do please come.'

Gina glanced at Ben. Surely he wouldn't want her to intrude? But he smiled. 'Mrs Swain has prepared a feast. Come and help us enjoy it ... today is your half-day, isn't it?'

'Please, Gina,' begged Harriet.

Unable to disappoint her pleading blue eyes, Gina smiled reluctantly. 'All right, I'll come, but I'm sure you would all rather eat alone.'

Audrey touched her arm lightly. 'I've waited weeks to meet you, Gina ... and I'm well aware of how busy a vet's life is. So I'm taking this opportunity to make the most of you. Come over when you're ready – on condition, of course, that we aren't taking you away from something else?'

Gina smiled and shook her head, telling herself that she must endeavour to endure being in Ben's company for the sake of Harriet and her grandmother. She had vowed to keep distanced, but at every turn it seemed she was thwarted ... making her decisions so much harder to bear.

She suppressed a shudder as she walked back to the surgery, suddenly remembering Vivienne and knowing with utter conviction that she had no wish to be put in the same category. Had Harriet mistakenly told her grandmother that there was a rival on the scene for Ben's affections? Teenagers had such colourful imaginations sometimes and she would not put it past Harriet to enlarge, in view of the girl's dislike for Vivienne.

Depressed by what she knew must be completely irrational thoughts, Gina found herself, an hour later, in front of the mirror, dressed in a long violet Indian-cotton skirt which matched her dark, glimmering eyes. She wondered why she had taken such trouble with her appearance if she had no wish to attract Ben's attention. Unable to answer her own question honestly, she sighed in confusion, running a last check over the sleeveless silk top which showed off her pale skin and small, high breasts and long, dark hair. She added a fine row of delicate Persian beads, smoothed creamy perfume on her wrists and slipped into light shoes which set off her small feet. As she walked, the cool spring air wafted around her long legs, the slim skirt clinging to the reed-like curves of her body.

'Hello!' Ben greeted her, smiling broadly as he opened the cottage door even before she knocked.

Forcing herself to react lightly, she smiled back.

He had changed from his suit and wore light trousers that accentuated the long, powerful length of his legs, and an open beige shirt displayed the deep brown skin of his neck scattered with dark whorls of hair. Her throat was dry and her stomach in a knot as he stared down at her. 'You look beautiful,' he said admiringly. 'It's such a lovely day we're sitting in the garden while Harriet makes some sense of Mrs Swain's instructions for lunch.'

'Perhaps I could give Harriet some help?' she volunteered.

'You could – but you won't!' He slipped a firm hand around her narrow waist, guiding her through the sunlit house and the French windows to the patio. Audrey sat under the shade of the apple trees on a canopied lounger. As they drew closer, she patted the seat beside her. 'You look so lovely, Gina!'

'That's exactly what I told her.' Ben grinned, his grey eyes catching hers for a brief second, but, swivelling on his heel as Gina sat down, he groaned. 'There's the phone ... back in a few minutes.'

'He's far too busy,' Audrey said with a sigh as they watched him go, his long strides taking him across the lawn. 'I do worry ... it's silly, but I can't help it.'

Gina nodded sympathetically. 'Yes, he is ... I think perhaps when I leave he may have to take on another vet permanently.'

Audrey frowned. 'Leave? But I thought–'

'My three-month contract is up in May,' Gina cut in gently but firmly.

'And you won't renew? Oh, dear...' Audrey sighed, resting back in her seat. 'I sound like an interfering old lady and we don't know one another very well ... but I was so hoping you were going to stay. Since Harriet has had you to talk to, she's a different girl. The transformation is startling, even during our conversations over the telephone each week.'

'If you mean her attitude towards animals...'

'No, not just animals,' Audrey said reflectively. 'You've given her a fresh outlook on life and somehow managed to persuade her out of the prejudices of the past. I haven't been blind to Harriet's problems and the fact that they stem from years back.'

Audrey paused, obviously finding it difficult to choose the right words. 'I loved

221

my daughter dearly, Gina, but the practice was everything to her. Often I assumed too much responsibility for my granddaughter. The truth is her mother took on far too many cases at the practice at the expense of time for Harriet ... and Ben. I should have been firmer, of course, but I saw the strain they were under and wanted to help – Sarah and Ben had a far from perfect marriage, you see.'

Gina was silent for a moment, unable to take in what Audrey had just said. 'But I thought ... I ... I had no idea...'

'Not many people did, even then,' Audrey explained with a sigh. 'Ben was a very loyal husband and a very private person. You see, my daughter was very wilful – as a child and a woman – a quality which often goes hand in hand with talent and dedication. Even on the night she died in that abysmal storm, Ben had warned her not to go out on her own. The conditions were treacherous. As it was, he wasn't at the surgery when the call was phoned in and, instead of waiting, Sarah took it into her own hands to attend. But that was Sarah ... and she paid the price – as we all did.' Audrey stared wearily into Gina's eyes. 'But especially Harriet. She must have felt cheated, and the way in which her mother died ... it all helped to alienate her against veterinary life.'

Gina took air into her lungs on a shocked

gasp. In her mind, she had built up Sarah to be a paragon of virtue. Yet she was just a woman with as many failings as any other, some of which had obviously affected her family so adversely that they bore the scars to this day.

It was hard to believe. But Audrey had made a great effort to enlighten her, at the expense of her own deeply cherished feelings.

'I'm sorry if I've embarrassed you in any way, my dear,' Audrey continued. 'But I wanted you to know the truth.' She gave Gina a perceptive stare, her tone grave. 'It's hard to live with ghosts, especially perfect ones. And we might not have the opportunity to have a heart-to-heart again if you are considering leaving. I've often wished I shared more with my daughter but there was never time ... so it seemed vital to me to give you some sort of insight into Ben and Harriet's past. I do hope I haven't offended you by talking so intimately?'

Stunned, Gina managed a smile. 'Of course not.'

As the older woman tactfully slipped into another subject, Gina hardly heard. She had listened to new truths and, if she was to believe them, to what degree had she misinterpreted Ben's feelings for his dead wife?

It was hard after that to concentrate on lunch, though she made the best of it that she could. Though Gina felt relief that Ben's feelings for Sarah could be viewed in a completely different light, that still left Vivienne. Had Vivienne in fact persuaded Ben that, despite his resolution not to remarry, marriage to her was a viable alternative? This could not be ruled out. It was all very well, Gina reflected, to have Audrey's and Harriet's support, but were they aware of how far his involvement had gone with Vivienne?

These questions seemed unanswerable as she politely ate her meal. Her own personal dislike for the woman had coloured her feelings. Vivienne was probably exactly the type of woman Ben desired; she had no challenging ambitions career-wise, and would make a tirelessly attentive companion and the perfect veterinary's wife.

During coffee the telephone rang and Harriet went to answer it. 'Gina … it's Lyn on the phone!' she called from the hall. 'Your enteritis case … he's having a fit!'

Gina hurriedly finished her coffee, vaguely registering her relief at being set free from Ben's grey gaze watching her intently across the table.

'Audrey, I'm terribly sorry,' she apologised. 'Dandy is rather a special case.'

'Naturally … please go.' Audrey smiled softly. 'And good luck with him. I hope it's nothing too serious.'

Harriet had already engrossed her grandmother in conversation as Gina left the room. Aware that Ben was shadowing her, she was further surprised when they reached the wicket gate and he pulled it open to follow her through. 'I'm coming with you,' he muttered.

'If you insist, but I can–'

He glanced warningly at her through lowered lids and, finding him striding stubbornly beside her, she decided not to argue.

They found Lyn in the recovery-room wiping the mongrel's panting black mouth. 'I thought it was a fit, but I'm not so sure now; the trouble is I can't hold him still!'

Ben knelt beside the nurse, taking over, his large hands going slowly over the dog's gullet. 'Gina, can you examine his throat ... around this area? I think I can feel a lump there.'

She grabbed a spatula and, in spite of Dandy's sharp nails accidentally grazing her bare arms, she managed to lay his tongue down. 'Yes! Something's lodged right at the back ... I'll try to get hold of it.'

Lyn handed her the forceps. She inserted them, but the dog gagged and she was forced to withdraw. Next time, though, she managed to clamp them over the object, pulling it out slowly.

'It looks like a ball of fur and it's anchored itself by a thread over a back tooth,' she murmured, trying to identify the dark shape. A final tug and the soggy ball was freed, caught firmly in the forceps. 'His throat's slightly infected and swollen.' She frowned as she placed the offending article in tissue. 'An injection of antibiotic, I think, Lyn.'

Ben meanwhile examined the tissue. 'A broken piece of tooth in the middle of the wet hair.' He sighed. 'The rascal's been having a feast licking his long fur and the tooth must have snapped. Probably because he hasn't eaten properly he finds it particularly difficult to swallow.'

Gina checked the measured quantity of antibiotic in the syringe and, while Ben distracted the dog, slid the needle into the muscle, massaging the area quickly. With just a little yelp, Dandy shivered and shook himself back on to his four paws.

'Poor little fellow.' Gina opened her arms and he crawled into them.

'You're hurt, Gina!' Ben ran his fingers over the ugly red weals on her smooth skin as she cuddled the dog.

She shook her head, shrugging off his concern. Her pretty silk blouse was covered in saliva and hair, but she laughed ruefully. 'All in a day's work – and Dandy's OK, which is the important thing.'

'You're important!' Ben contradicted, frowning at her. 'Let Lyn put Dandy back in his recovery cage with a drink and I'll clean up those scratches for you.'

Lyn took Dandy in her arms. 'By the way, Mr Forsythe phoned again ... he would like you to ring him, Ben.'

'Again?' Ben looked surprised.

'He called this morning about Chamois,' Gina explained, suddenly remembering the call. 'I left a message on your desk, but with Audrey arriving you probably didn't get around to seeing it. Chamois is showing improvement ... but I had a feeling he wanted to talk to you about another matter.'

'I'll ring him all in good time. First I'm going to bathe those wounds.' Ben helped her to her feet, his large hand slipping around her waist, and her mouth went dry at the sensation he sent rippling through her body.

Her wounds were superficial, but he insisted on leading her into the dispensary where he collected antiseptic and lint and made her sit down as he treated her. With great care he began to clean the lesions, which were just beginning to burn, but, for Gina, the torture of watching him at such close quarters was far worse than the cleaning of the scratches.

Without him knowing she stared into the thickness of his dark, glossy hair, smelling the familiar musky aftershave which he used. He was such a large man, tall and tough-looking, but so graceful in his movements.

Her eyes lingered hungrily on his fingers, lean and brown with sculptured short nails. Dark coils of hair sprang at his wrist and wound up his powerful forearm until they disappeared under the short-sleeved shirt.

She felt his delicate touch with a kind of breathless panic. His grey eyes came up to meet hers, tender in their slate depths, so deep and mysterious. She had grown to know him well, to know all the curves and juts of his strong features, the powerful thrust of chin which so reflected his character. But she had never known what had been going on in that mind, never once guessed he had anything but an idyllic marriage to Sarah.

She made no move as he bent to kiss her.

It was a gentle, slow kiss, his mouth lingering only a moment. She felt dazed, her heart leaping as though she had jumped across a deep chasm. She was drowned first in pleasure and then, as he kissed her again, in pain. The discovery that he still wasn't holding a candle for Sarah did not remove the fact that he was still seeing Vivienne. She could hardly take his advances seriously if this was so!

She stiffened, pulling away, feeling the unbearable chill of emptiness and despair sweep over her.

Frowning, he lowered her arm to her lap, sliding his fingertips along the skin lightly.

'I'll ring Jake,' he said with equal stiffness, turning to the washbasin, wiping his hands briskly, and then, pausing briefly to glance at her, he strode from the room.

Gina sat alone, enclosed in a thick, heavy shroud of depression. She wasn't aware of how long she was lost in the mood, only coming back to earth when she heard Stuart's voice, realising he had come in for his three o'clock surgery. She stood up quickly as he strolled through the door.

'Gina! What's happened to your arm?' he asked worriedly. 'And what are you doing here? It's your afternoon off, isn't it?'

She nodded. 'We came across to see Dandy. He had an obstruction in his throat.'

'He put up a good fight by the looks of it. Have you had those scratches treated?'

She nodded as Ben came into the room.

'You here too?' Stuart grinned. 'I missed all the excitement again!'

They sat and talked for a while, the warmth of the afternoon conducive to the usual remarks about the forthcoming summer. Gina's mind refused to let the memory of Ben's kiss vanish. Emotion flooded her with unexpected force as she thought of it, her pulses picking up pace as every now and then she caught Ben's grey gaze and subsequently lost the thread of the conversation. Deciding it was time to make a departure before she gave herself away, she rose a little unsteadily. 'If you don't need any help this afternoon, Stuart, I'll be going.'

To her relief, the young vet shook his head. 'Of course not. Make the most of what's left of the afternoon. I'll keep an eye on Dandy.'

Gina smiled gratefully. 'Thanks. I'll give him some more antibiotic in the morning, but if you would take another look at his throat after surgery–'

'No problem,' Stuart cut in, ushering her onwards. 'Just stop worrying and put your feet up.'

Ben walked with her through Reception and out into the sunshine. 'Good advice,' he said as they neared the cottage. 'About putting your feet up, I mean. Though, knowing you as I do, I'm quite sure you won't take it.'

She half smiled, aware of his closeness, the broad shoulders moving beside her, the tilt of his dark head as he looked down at her. A pang of love engulfed her, love that had been dammed up for so long and which she couldn't express. The afternoon was no longer warm and in the distance, over the fields, a dewy haze rolled over the landscape, heralding evening, making her unhappiness twist like a dagger in her heart.

They stopped at the wicket gate and she hesitated, almost afraid to look up into his eyes. When she did, he was staring at her, his gaze unfathomable. 'How do you feel about coming in and having the cup of tea we never got around to?' Then, at her reluctance to reply, he frowned at her arm and added quickly, 'But I don't suppose you're feeling up to it.'

'No, no, it's not that...' She felt suddenly tired, tired of trying to think coherently. 'I must visit my parents before Easter. Perhaps I'll go while the roads are still fairly reasonable. I shall be on call over the holiday and I don't want to have it on my mind that I haven't seen them.'

'Not all the holiday!' he corrected, his eyes suddenly sharp. 'I've decided. You're covering Good Friday only; Stuart can work Saturday and Sunday because he took last weekend off. And I'm going to cover Monday.'

'But ... what about the garden party?' she reminded him, frowning deeply.

'I'll have the bleeper for the nurses to call me if I'm needed.' He paused, staring at her with brooding grey eyes. 'Besides, I might ask you the same thing. You're going with Kieron Brent, aren't you? I don't imagine he would appreciate your being whisked away from under his nose as the result of an emergency call-out.'

Gina's mouth parted on a gasp, her words of protest lost as Audrey appeared at the door of the cottage and drew their attention. 'Ben, you're wanted on the telephone,' she called, then mouthed to Gina, 'Sorry to interrupt!'

231

Ben raised a large brown hand. 'Coming, Audrey!'

'But Ben–!' Gina managed, only to see him move away, casting her one last, cold stare.

With a shrug of dismissal he went, pushed through the wicket gate and hurried towards the cottage without a backward glance.

CHAPTER ELEVEN

There could only be one person, Gina decided, who would tell Ben such a thing. Vivienne.

All thoughts of enjoying the remainder of her afternoon off now faded. The rest of the day passed in a blur, her anger turning to a deep frustration. She considered ringing Vivienne, but a warning inner voice prevented her. Vivienne was an expert in this field of deception and she had no wish to compete. If Ben was taken in by her each time, well, in a few weeks it wouldn't matter, anyway...

The following day, though she had made up her mind to dismiss the idea of trying to put things right with Ben, she barely saw him in surgery. For the most part, she checked the animals in the recovery-room and worked with Stuart in order that, over the Easter holiday, there were few boarders for the nurses to care for.

Dandy's owner came to collect him and, apart from his misadventure the day before, he seemed fit enough to leave.

'I would like you to carry on with this diet.' Gina led Dandy from his cage and returned him to the young woman. He went into a furious licking bout and she swept him up into her arms with delight. 'I want him to have plenty of proteins and carbohydrates,' Gina emphasised, 'and I'll give you some vitamins to supplement, too. He's also on antibiotics so he will need supervising quite closely. I'd like to see him in a month's time – before, if you've any problems.'

The young woman nodded. 'I can see why it's so risky to buy a dog on the spur of the moment now. He looks so much better!'

Gina hesitated. 'It's very important to give a lot of thought to offering a dog a home. Luckily Dandy has you as a caring owner, but if, as you say, he looked poorly soon after you acquired him, the possibility is that the other dogs he lived with had an infection too. That's why it's so important to go to a reputable breeder.'

'Wise after the event,' sighed the girl, stroking the soft black crown. 'But the house has been terribly quiet. I wouldn't be without him.'

Gina smiled. 'I'm glad it all worked out.'

'I'll make an appointment now … and I don't have to work until next Wednesday so my husband and I are going to be with him all the time.'

Gina was relieved. Dandy had become a favourite with the staff, his fight for survival showing he had a courageous heart inside a fragile little body. He deserved to make a good recovery.

By the afternoon, the holiday atmosphere pervaded the waiting-room, just a few stragglers left with their pets, mostly cats and dogs with minor ailments and requiring boosters before the long weekend.

Julian called in for one of his rare visits to see Ben who had hardly emerged from the office all day, immersed in his paperwork. After Julian left, wishing them all a happy Easter, Ben passed her in the hall, merely nodding.

She felt there was nothing for it but to accept the situation. Whatever happened, she was determined to avoid any argument and try, somehow, to see out the remainder of her time here peacefully. And no matter how she felt about Ben she had to keep a sense of perspective and remember that she had almost allowed herself to make one disastrous mistake before which could have ruined her life. She might not have been able to prevent herself from falling in love with Ben, but that didn't mean she was bereft of the strength to fight it!

With her mind focused with determination on her last client, a well-built man with reddish hair, she paid little attention to Harriet's expression as she showed the client into her room.

The man had a large dog called Ziggy, a

mastiff he had brought over from France, which was just out of quarantine. He asked Gina to examine the dog thoroughly as a second opinion besides that of the kennels he had been isolated in. He was a beautiful animal, good ears and eyes and a strong heart and obviously well looked after. Gina had no hesitation in giving Ziggy a clean bill of health.

Harriet came into her room after the client had gone. Gina smiled, unable to resist the lure of Harriet's searching gaze. 'I give in.' She laughed. 'You're bursting to tell me something, aren't you?'

Harriet nodded, abandoning her half-hearted attempt at cleaning down the treatment table. 'Didn't you recognise him?'

Gina frowned. 'Who ... the man with the mastiff? Should I?'

'That's Mr Armitage! He's come back to live in England, after his business failed in France. Didn't you know?'

Gina shook her head. 'No. I've never met him before.'

'I think–' Harriet carried on unflinchingly, 'that the night Vivienne came to us in floods of tears over an argument she had with him was just to get Daddy's sympathy.'

Gina frowned, her heart racing, curious despite herself.

'We let her stay in the spare room, because she said she was frightened he might cause trouble at the farm. She was crying all over the place, saying Mr Armitage was angry at the way she hoodwinked him out of the farm and he had ended up with nothing. Poor Daddy didn't know what to do with her.'

Vivienne Armitage had slept overnight in the guest room? Could it be true...? But it was hardly likely that Harriet would make up such a story!

'Vivienne tries everything to get Daddy's attention, you see ... but he just feels sorry for her,' Harriet concluded with a sigh.

Gina felt her blood run cold. 'You mean Vivienne isn't...?' Blushing deeply, she tried to avoid Harriet's eyes but it was too late – the girl had registered her shock and embarrassment.

'She's not Daddy's girlfriend, no!' Harriet supplied astutely. 'Not for the want of trying, though! She likes to give people the impression – if you see what I mean?'

Gina knew what Harriet meant – only too well. And she had fallen for every cunning twist and turn to Vivienne's little plots, right from the beginning.

'Oh, dear.' Harriet sighed, her blue eyes suddenly anxious. 'I'm getting as bad as Mrs Swain for gossip!'

Gina managed a hesitant smile. She had to have time to think! But, almost on cue, Ben walked in, his eyes flashing momentarily as he sensed the atmosphere. 'Harriet, can you take the remaining two dogs in Recovery for short walks? Their owners are coming at six to take them home, so I would like it done before then, please.'

Harriet nodded, grinning at Gina as she escaped.

Ben remained, staring at her in silence. Had he seen Reggie Armitage and his Ziggy? If he had he gave no sign as he dug his hands deeply in his pockets, resting a thigh on the edge of her desk. 'The roster's confirmed. You're on call tomorrow – Friday. Stuart has Saturday and Sunday.'

'But I'm quite happy to cover the whole weekend...' she began, only to stop as his expression darkened.

'I can hardly believe that – you'll want time off with Brent.'

Kieron again! 'I'm not seeing Kieron,' she retorted as her heart beat violently. This time she was not going to keep quiet; she was going to tell Ben exactly what Vivienne was trying to do, for there was no point in allowing the malicious woman to get away with further mischief-making. 'Ben, despite what you may have been given to understand, I'd like to put the record straight–'

'Let's just forget it, shall we?' he cut in abruptly, shifting off the desk and moving towards the door.

'You want to forget an issue when it's

convenient for you.' She gasped in anger, forcing him to turn back. 'Yet when I choose to try to clear up certain misunderstandings you won't give me the time of day. I hardly think you're being fair!'

'Fair?' His dark eyebrows shot up. 'Heavens above, Gina, I've tried to be fair all along the line with you.' He snapped his jaw to. 'Damn it! If you're involved with the guy, then why not admit it? Some women have no choice whom they fall for. I don't blame you for something you can't stop, but why deny it any longer?'

'I'm not denying anything – because there is nothing to deny!' she flew at him. 'Kieron and I were never ... we weren't involved – and we aren't now!'

'Then why is he pursuing you?' he demanded with quiet scorn. 'You must have encouraged him or he wouldn't still be part of your life. And if you must know ... I talked to him, the night he brought you home.'

'You ... talked to him?' she asked uneasily.

'Just before he got in his car. I asked him what the hell was going on and he didn't like it one little bit. Told me it was none of my damn business; you were his girlfriend and I should leave you alone.'

'But that's simply not true!'

'And then there's Monday,' he carried on, his face growing red with anger. 'When Viv told me you were coming as a couple, I decided you were making it public enough how things stood. But I just couldn't understand why you lied to me!'

'I ... I haven't lied!' Gina stammered. 'You must believe me. It isn't me who is lying, it's—' She stopped before she made the accusation, her lips quivering.

He would never believe her suspicions about Vivienne or the truth about Kieron, the mood he was in. There was only one thing she could do and that was to let him cool down.

To think she loved a man who accused her of being able to lie with such distinction – and for what reason? To tease two men at the same time? To pander to her sense of vanity? Was that what he really thought of her?

Hurt beyond measure, she gripped the windowsill with trembling fingers staring blindly out of the window, aware that her feelings were a potent mixture of anger and injustice.

'You can't have it both ways, Gina,' he said, to cap it all.

The words rang in her ears along with the angry pulse that almost obliterated the voice of one of the girls from Reception calling his name.

When finally she'd gathered herself enough to turn around he'd vanished.

She stared at the vacant space, her heart

hammering. Why couldn't she get through to him? Her eyes smarted with unshed tears as she thought of the light in which he regarded her. Whichever way she turned, it seemed hopeless.

On Easter Saturday she visited her parents, trying resolutely to form some picture of a future in her mind. Another practice somewhere; perhaps she should try the north of England. She had a few ties in the Dales ... perhaps this was the perfect opportunity...

She felt better as she drove through the Purbecks, the sun glinting on the hills with the promise of summer and a future. She would forget Ben ... and Harriet ... and the practice she had grown to love...

In time, this heartache would resolve itself.

The day that she was dreading arrived – Easter Monday.

Cloudless blue skies stretched to the horizon, birds sang in the garden and a warm breeze stirred the first early buds on the trees.

All this ... and a feeling of utter despondency! At her parents' Gina had been unable to relax, feeling tense, and it was no better at home.

She would face the day alone, make sure she busied herself with spring-cleaning,

241

anything to occupy her mind. At eleven, she had just thrown on an apron over her jeans and red shirt and was trying to decide on where she should begin to vacuum when Harriet burst in.

Dressed in striped Bermuda shorts and a T-shirt, she proclaimed, 'Guess what? One of the kittens ran under Nana's feet and she's twisted her ankle so she won't be able to go to Vivienne's!' With a rueful grin, she added in a whisper, 'Not that she's disappointed!' Harriet eyed the apron in disgust. 'I just came in to say goodbye.'

'You're not going with your father?' Gina asked in surprise.

Harriet grinned. 'I got out of it. Jenny's parents offered to have me to stay until Thursday, then I'll be back to help in surgery.' Affectionately, Harriet gave her a hug. 'Happy Easter, Gina!'

She was so surprised, she simply followed Harriet out into the garden and, as the trendy shorts disappeared into the back of Jenny's father's estate wagon, waved her goodbye.

'Well, aren't you getting ready for the garden party?' said a deep voice from the next garden.

She spun around to see Ben, gazing at her.

She shot him a glacial look. 'I'm not going to one!'

He frowned, staring at her, dark eyebrows

shadowing the grey eyes. 'Really? But I thought–'

'If you had listened to me when I was trying to explain,' she said, struggling to maintain her composure, 'you would know by now that I never did have any intention whatsoever of going to Vivienne's garden party!' She paused, taking a deep breath relishing his sudden discomfort and confusion at this new piece of information.

He nodded slowly, regarding her through lowered lids. 'Oh! I see.'

'Vivienne told you I was going with Kieron Brent and you believed her!' she reminded him scathingly.

Ben nodded. 'I'm afraid I did.'

'Well, I–'

'Vivienne has said,' Ben interrupted firmly, 'and done rather a lot of strange things lately, so I've discovered. For instance, Harry tells me she overheard that I was lined up as a prospective candidate for husband number two and Audrey informs me she had a phone call a week or so back reminding her of … "our" garden party.'

Delicious white teeth emerged slowly from widely parted lips. 'Er … which reminds me, you've heard the news, I suppose, that Audrey's sprained an ankle?'

A few minutes later, minus her apron, temper defused, Gina found herself sitting with Audrey amid a slight sense of dazedness, sipping Earl Grey in the front room of the cottage, having been persuaded in by a thoughtful Ben.

Audrey, with her ankle neatly wrapped in a support bandage, sighed contentedly. 'So unfortunate! Now I shall be forced to sit and read a novel and drink tea all day in the tranquillity of the garden.'

Gina laughed, her violet eyes soft, her hair coiling in dark ringlets around her face.

'You know ... you look hardly older than Harriet, my dear,' Audrey said reflectively. 'I don't know how your male colleagues manage to keep their minds on their work!'

The compliment was generous, Gina thought gratefully, but desirability hardly seemed important any more; in fact maybe people's appearances were sometimes a disadvantage where true love was concerned.

She gazed out of the cottage window wistfully – and nearly dropped her cup! Ben's tall figure leaned casually at the wicket gate and he was talking to a fair-haired man ... a few inches shorter ... Kieron!

'Gina ... what's the matter? You've gone as white as a sheet.'

'Oh...' She swallowed hard, jumping to her feet to get a closer look. There was no mistake. 'Ben is talking to...'

'Someone from the practice?' Audrey asked inquisitively.

'Well ... he is a vet, a colleague I worked

with at my first practice in Surrey.' Gina hesitated. 'I wonder what he's talking to Ben about?'

'Should you go and see, do you think?'

Gina turned back and sat down heavily, her heart thumping. Should she? What was going on out there? And why was Kieron here, unless...?

Audrey leaned forward, touching her hand lightly. 'Ben will bring him in, I'm sure.'

Gina wasn't altogether sure of that. They looked deep in conversation, Ben's brow intent as Kieron talked to him.

She tried to control her growing inner panic. The last person she wanted to bump into today was Kieron Brent. Going out there would only mean she would be drawn into an argument. If they both decided to come in, of course, it would be a different matter...

Ten very long minutes later, she heard Ben's footfall. All her perceptions seemed heightened as she listened to him approaching – her heartbeat, the silence of the cottage on a beautiful spring morning, Audrey's soft breathing.

When she swivelled in her seat, Ben was standing at the door, his large frame filling it.

'It's a glorious day,' he said, quite calmly. 'You'll enjoy the garden, Audrey – far nicer than where we plan to spend the next hour or two.'

'We?' Gina repeated hesitantly.

'Yes, you and I.' Ben walked towards her, leaned down, took her hands and lifted her to her feet. 'Go and change into the prettiest dress you have in your wardrobe and, in exactly one hour, be ready to come with me. No arguments! Not a word! Just do as you're told. Because if you don't I shall come in and carry you off dressed as you are. Do you understand?'

She swallowed, her violet eyes wide in protest. 'No … I don't think I do!'

He slid an arm around her waist and propelled her towards the hall. She just managed to turn and wave goodbye to a smiling Audrey.

'Trust me,' he whispered to her when they arrived at the front door. 'For once, just trust me, Gina.'

As she showered and dressed, she wondered why she was so obediently following his instructions. Spring madness perhaps? He had asked her to trust him. Her heart beat violently with apprehension, though. What could be in his mind and where, exactly, was he taking her and what had he said to Kieron?

She regarded herself in the mirror. Her hands were trembling … a symptom of the panic she felt inside. But the result of her labours was surprising. Glossy, ebony hair tumbling freely over her shoulders, a hint of mascara and a dash of lipstick. Her skin had begun to darken even with the small amount of sun and her eyes glimmered from their depths ... purple-violet in their unquestionable hue.

She wore a dress of deep violet, cut with a simple round neckline, curving over her small breasts, moulding to every gentle curve of her slender figure. Nothing elaborate but, in its simplicity, quite stunning.

Her parents had given her a single-string pearl choker. It lay delicately against the soft creaminess of her skin, the only embellishment necessary to make the ensemble perfect.

When she opened the door to Ben, his face seemed frozen in surprise as his eyes wandered slowly over her. Tall and dark and more handsome than ever in an elegant grey suit, he stood in silence for a few seconds staring at her.

'Gina!' he whispered and without hesitating swept her into his arms. She went unresistingly, knowing in that moment that every decision was made for her. Her desire of him, her need was too great to be denied any longer and her arms slipped around his neck as a sob of relief seemed to come from way down deep inside.

As he kissed her, her heart throbbed with a love she would never be able to quench.

The flame of passion burnt so brightly, nothing would put out the fire. And if that was all there was ... so be it! Life would be desolate when he left her, when it was over, but she would take the risk. She couldn't stop now...

She gazed up at him in a daze, her mouth softly bruised by the intensity of their kiss. 'Are you ready?' he asked with a smile that made her heart turn over.

'I'm ready,' she answered softly.

The drive to Vivienne's seemed like a dream!

Gina sat beside him in silence, her thoughts anaesthetised by the knowledge that she was with him and that was all that mattered. The future could take care of itself, she told herself recklessly; she was his, for as long as he wanted her.

The big house stood like a Christmas tree, decorated with streamers and flags and festoons draped from the windows. Cars were parked nose to bumper along the drive and Harvey walked past the Discovery, raising a new cloth-cap in welcome.

Ben came around and held up his hands and she felt them clasp tightly around her waist. He brought her slowly to the ground and she leaned into him, a small sigh escaping from her moist lips as he brushed a hand under her ebony hair, laying it softly on her shoulders.

'Do you think this is wise, Ben?' she asked, her voice barely above a whisper. 'I don't know why you've brought me here, but–'

He drew her to him. 'We're going to this damn garden party, come hell or high water!' His voice was hard, but his eyes travelled over her, expressing an inner message of hungry desire which overrode his sudden anger. 'I've been a fool,' he said huskily, his eyes greyer than she had ever seen them before.

Bewildered, she stared at him. 'Has this anything to do with Kieron, by any chance?'

He nodded. 'I'm afraid to say it has. He told me everything, right from the beginning. He's not such a bad guy; now I know there is nothing between you, I suppose I can afford to feel generous. Gina ... you'll have to forgive me. I was jealous as hell and I wouldn't listen to you.'

'You ... jealous?' Unable to bear the sadness in his eyes, she said quickly, 'There is nothing to forgive, Ben. I just don't understand why Kieron admitted the truth all of a sudden.'

'He's been feeling guilty about what he told me. And, knowing that he'd also been a party to Viv's scheming to keep us apart, he felt he had to put things right before the garden party this afternoon.' Frowning at her, he tilted up her chin. 'He also supplied me with vital information – information I should have had from you, Gina. Why didn't you tell me the doctors thought you might never practise again?'

So Kieron had told him about that too!

She closed her eyes briefly, trying to wipe out the awful memory, but Ben's strong fingers gripped her arms, giving her a little shake.

'Damn it, Gina! If you had told me the whole story it would have explained so much!'

She nodded. 'I didn't want you to pity me. I wanted the job on my own merit. It was just a battle with myself I was fighting, Ben, that was all.'

He sighed. 'If only you'd told me! I thought–'

'You thought I was an ambitious female obsessed with furthering my career, didn't you?'

He nodded slowly. 'But can you really blame me? Sarah and I ... we–'

Gina laid soft fingers across his mouth. 'You don't have to explain.'

He took hold of her hand. 'But I do have to explain; I want you to know. I needed more out of our marriage than careers. I've always wanted a home, kids, lots of them...' He shrugged. 'Sarah didn't. She loved her work; it was enough for her. Then, when I met you, I couldn't dissociate past from present. It was as though I was locked in a time-warp. I couldn't see you for the person you really are.'

He drew her into him, pressing her head to his hard chest, raking his fingers through her hair and kissing the top of her head.

'And how do you see me, Ben? What sort of woman do you think I am?' she asked him breathlessly.

He held her face between his hands. 'Apart from being the most beautiful girl I have ever set eyes on?' He smiled. 'Gina, you're the kind of woman I want to spend the rest of my life with. I'm in love with you, Gina ... deeply in love.'

'You're...' She shook her head in disbelief. 'Oh, Ben, I thought–'

'You thought I was having a raging affair with Vivienne, didn't you?' He grinned.

She tried to hide her scarlet cheeks, but he laughed and bent to kiss each of them softly.

'I understand, darling.' He hesitated, frowning, holding her tightly. 'Viv did everything to give you the wrong idea – even got hold of Brent's number and rang him in order to get him to bring you here today.'

Gina gazed up at him and her hands slid into his dark hair. 'Vivienne made it sound as if this garden party was to be given by you both,' she now had the courage to admit. 'I feel a fool for believing her now, but she was so convincing; in fact, I have to admire her, just a little.'

'I wouldn't waste your time,' Ben whispered reprovingly, kissing the tip of her nose. 'We're going in there, you and I, and we're going to make this a day to remember!'

She grinned up at him. 'A turn of the screw?'

He shook his head. 'No, not revenge, just unbelievable relief. We may not have been standing here now if Vivienne's call hadn't pricked our mutual friend's conscience. You see, Kieron also told me he thought you had fallen in love with someone else...'

They were silent for a while, staring at one another, hearts beating hard at the implication of his incomplete sentence. Then Gina gave a little gasp of sudden understanding and hot colour flooded her face as tears of joy spilled down her cheeks.

'Now I want you to tell me,' he ordered gently, wiping them away with a large brown finger so soft on her cheek. 'Tell me you love me, Gina. Say you'll be my wife?'

'Your–!' She had no time to repeat the word as he kissed her again, deeply, passionately, sliding his strong hands possessively around her, rendering her powerless except to whisper over and over in between kisses, 'I love you... I love you, Ben.'

Her heart was overflowing. She thought it might burst as she gasped for air. Then, recalling every word in detail over the last five incredible minutes, she murmured, 'Children? Did you say … children?'

He drew her closer, tighter in his strong arms. 'Have you any objections?' His voice was thick as he threaded his fingers through her tumbling hair.

'Harriet,' she murmured softly. 'Do you think she'll be happy for us?'

'Delirious!' He grinned. 'I don't think we'll have to do much explaining.'

'Oh, Ben … do you mean that?'

'Harry's been streets ahead of us for light-years.' He laughed. 'Aren't most kids, when it comes down to reading their parents like open books?'

Her lips were but a fraction away from his when the small instrument hidden in his breast pocket bleeped shrilly.

They looked into one another's eyes and began to laugh. 'Intuition tells me,' Ben said slowly, 'that we are destined never to make our sweeping entrance at Vivienne's garden party.' He sighed deeply, drinking her in. 'I don't want to let you out of my arms, but I'll have to ring the surgery…'

She nodded, her face flushed with love. 'Of course you will – and you'll have to go.'

'*We* will have to go,' he emphasised, lifting her back into the Discovery before she could say a word more. 'I'm certainly not leaving you here! Kindred spirits always stay together; didn't you know that?'

No; she had only dared to hope it, she thought silently, ecstatically, as she watched him close her door. And hope had won.

Love had won.

Their love!

When he was beside her and the call back to surgery was made, he leaned across, wrapping her in his arms. 'Sounds like it might be a Caesarean.'

'Our first together,' she murmured, drowning in the magic of his deep voice.

'The first of – many arrivals,' he agreed with a twist of irony.

And, as his mouth closed over hers in breathless promise of their future, Gina knew that her dreams – every single one – would all come true.

The publishers hope that this book has given you enjoyable reading. Large Print Books are especially designed to be as easy to see and hold as possible. If you wish a complete list of our books please ask at your local library or write directly to:

Dales Large Print Books
Magna House, Long Preston,
Skipton, North Yorkshire.
BD23 4ND

This Large Print Book, for people
who cannot read normal print,
is published under the auspices of

THE ULVERSCROFT FOUNDATION

... we hope you have enjoyed this book.
Please think for a moment about those
who have worse eyesight than you ...
and are unable to even read or enjoy
Large Print without great difficulty.

You can help them by sending a
donation, large or small, to:

**The Ulverscroft Foundation,
1, The Green, Bradgate Road,
Anstey, Leicestershire, LE7 7FU,
England.**
or request a copy of our brochure for
more details.

The Foundation will use all donations
to assist those people who are visually
impaired and need special attention
with medical research, diagnosis
and treatment.

Thank you very much for your help.